ENDLESS

LIVING

ORGAN

MASSACRE

DEREK
HEATH

Pope Lick Press
© 2024

PART I

TUNNELS

OF

GORE

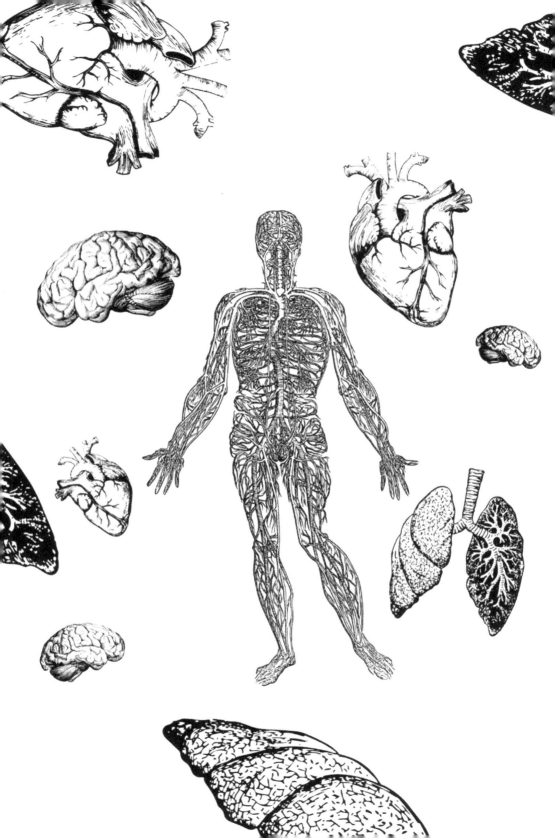

1

The thing lay still, pulsing wetly, seven or eight feet from where he sat sprawled against the basement wall. It was about the size and shape of a half-deflated basketball, coated with a thick, glutinous membrane that shimmered in the spotlight of a flickering fluorescent lamp on the ceiling. Pinkish and shrivelled, parts of the thing were stretched over bulbous solid masses while others sagged loosely into shallow, bubbling sockets. White-blue veins spread over its surface in a gleaming network of throbbing colour. It breathed softly.

The basement was dark and grotty, illuminated only by spots of dim amber where more square pitches of fluorescence punched their greasy knuckles into the concrete. The walls were piled high with heaps of deformed shadow. Clumps of gloss-coated things sloped up into the cobwebs and dust-vines that swung from the ceiling in the soft breeze of a stuttering fan. Fat, sharp blades behind a thick iron grille cast billowing, sharp-edged shadows against the opposite wall as they spun. The basement echoed with the whining whirr of the machine.

Something moved.

The young man groaned, knees cracking loudly beneath him as he tried to stand. His body was stiff. Immediately he reached for his stomach, grunting as he clamped a hand over the malnourished pouch of flesh at his waist. He felt weak and hungry, his throat dry and coarse. A wall of vertigo smashed into him as he straightened up and he stumbled backward, tripping over something small and sharp. His back slammed hard into the wall and he slid down it again, bones rattling in a thin casing of muscles that felt stringy and useless.

A fat bead of warmth seeped across the sole of the young man's bare foot and he cringed as the pain-heat spread. Glancing down between his legs to discern what he'd stepped on, he saw it: a fragment of bone, about the size of a knuckle and chipped at the edges. One particularly ragged corner was dotted with his blood.

"Ow," he said groggily.

Hands splayed in front of him, the boy squinted through a haze of sleep and half-heartedly looked himself over. He was naked and dirty, his groin and stomach smeared with dry blood. His legs and arms were bruised and a thick clot of yellow-purple stained his left side. His ribs poked out against the thin flesh of his chest.

He was a bony, thin white wraith of a figure, angular joints bulging beneath taut and translucent skin. Patches of his body were red-raw, as though the outer layers of flesh had been scraped away to reveal the striated meat beneath, and the edges of these patches were discoloured yellow. He thought, rather sharply, that he looked like a rotting fruit: the pale white of his skin was like a pastel-blue clump of moss-mould which had spread across the shining, blotchy crimson of his body, and though it hadn't covered him entirely yet, he knew that he wasn't fit for consumption. He remembered... nothing. Nothing of substance, just bolts of colour. Explosions of sound.

He was in the library when they took him.

His head pounded. Heart fluttering weakly in his chest, he rolled his skull on a neck that crunched audibly. Drew in a long, deep breath of stale air. *The library.* How long ago had that been? He remembered thick-fingered hands crushing his wrists, more of them snaking out of the space behind him and clamping around his neck. Remembered the cold spike of a needle sliding between gloved fingers into his carotid

and pumping something cool and thick into him, remembered a gentle hushing in his ear, and then—

Here.

The basement was enormous, a vast cavern of concrete and shadow. The walls were smeared with throbbing veins of light, like rivers of wet copper running through the grit and charcoal of some abandoned mineshaft. The concrete was a dull, dark shade of blue and in places thick brass pipes poked out of the walls and ran up into the ceiling. Gargantuan pillars and archways exploded from the ground, covered with moss and tangled in long, interlocking trails of ivy. Blossoms of fungus plumed from bright patches of slurry filth, the crests of fat, shallow mushrooms painted a gloriously bright yellow in the dark.

The sloping mounds of viscera around him were indistinguishable in the dim, flickering light, but he knew what they were. The smell was incredible.

Hot, ripe fruit and urine.

Blood.

Insides.

There was a sudden *kunk-unk-unk* from far above him and his eyes shot up, drawn quickly to a thin crescent of glacier-white light in the very centre of the ceiling. As he watched, the crescent swung around a pitch-black axis like a bulb on a cable, flitting left to right with a clatter of metal and growing slimmer, slimmer until – finally – it filled with black.

As his eyes continued to adjust to the dark he saw that the space where the crescent had been was not entirely black, but glinted like metal in the fluttering fluorescent lights.

Some kind of trapdoor, he realised, a hatch. Perhaps a manhole cover. A long, narrow ladder descended from the ceiling, still shivering – vibrating like a tuning fork – with the memory of whatever had climbed it and escaped through the opening. If only he had looked up, just moments before, he might have caught a glimpse of it before it disappeared, closing the lid behind it.

Only half-consciously, he was glad he'd missed it.

Eventually his gaze was drawn back to the ground, and to the pulsing fleshy thing that lay deflated only a couple of yards from him. He had been avoiding it, assuming it was some kind of half-dead animal, but now that he had semi-assessed the rest of the basement he found that his curiosity was uncomfortably piqued. He had to look. To know.

Slowly, carefully, he clambered to his knees. Bracing himself with both hands against the wall behind him, he eased himself into a crooked standing position. His legs felt as though they'd never been used, his arms just as weak. He stood there panting for a moment, dark spots dancing in front of his eyes. At least the thing that had climbed the ladder had *left* the basement, he thought, rather than coming *in* here with him.

As he padded forward, his eyes flickered upward and he noted a wide, steel door in the opposite wall, standing atop a pair of chipped concrete stairs. Swinging his neck, the young man looked around and saw a second door to his right, this one bulging and round-cornered like a door in a submarine – complete with an enormous, metal wheel in its centre.

Dust pressed into the bloody mess of his heel as he moved toward the throbbing basketball-sized thing. Every step was painful and slow, and he kept his hand pressed to his stomach as he walked. Squinting, he bent forward to look down.

His breath hitched in his throat as he realised what he was looking at.

"Oh," he moaned, his vocal cords too painful to produce any more than that faint grunt of protest. If his heart wasn't smashing his ribs so hard he might have been able to curse. Instead, he turned his head back and bent over double, vomiting thin strings onto the floor until his mouth burned with the acidic taste. Emptied, he tipped his head back and croaked.

When he returned his attention to the thing on the concrete, it had moved slightly.

"*Ohh...*"

At first he had thought it was a single lung, bloated and deformed and lumpy, but after a brief and reluctant assessment he realised that it was a *pair* of lungs, fused messily together, one knitted into the fabric of the other so that they became one sickening clump of pink tissue. A network of tubes flopped about on the thing's underside, working like sinuous red tentacles to drag it slowly across the concrete. He could only see their tips beneath mounds of throbbing blue muscle but he could hear them, wetly slapping each other as they moved, pulling it forward, pulling it *toward* him—

The boy swallowed back more vomit and lurched past the deformed fleshy thing, stumbling into the middle of the room. He grabbed the ladder as he passed it to steady himself, momentarily considering climbing it – then remembering that something else had left that way only minutes before, something that he wasn't entirely desperate to encounter. Heading for the steel door at the far end of the room, he remembered the shapeless mounds that surrounded him and realised he'd been avoiding looking at them, perhaps already aware what he might see. Before he could stop himself he glanced down into the nearest shadowy heap and saw chips of bone scattered among larger pieces, ribs poking out of the dark, greasy sheets of skin punctured and hanging loosely between knobs of throbbing muscle and bruised pieces of skull.

The basement was filled with remains. Human remains. The flesh and muscle were scattered and scraped few and far between, but the *bones*...

Finally reaching the wall, he laid both hands on the door and bowed his head to catch his breath. He had to get out of here. He didn't know why they'd brought him here, why they'd dumped him in this grotty cave of bones and weird conjoined-lung abominations, but he had to get *out*.

He looked up and a face stared back at him through the greasy glass of a round, reinforced window in the door.

The face was haunted and white, eyes sunk into deep pits, hair ragged and dark and thin. Stubble covered its chin and jaw, cracked lips parted slightly, breath pluming on the glass like fog. He stepped back, and the face behind the glass sunk back into the dark.

It was him. His reflection.

Breathing a sigh of relief, he looked himself up and down. Remembered. He was a person. He had a life; a name. He had always been tall for his age – when he was fifteen, he had towered over some of the others in his year at school – but now his frame was hunched a little, his back and shoulders crooked as though a great weight had slammed into him and permanently disfigured his skeleton. His testicles were shrivelled with the cold and his joints were blue with it. He needed to find something to wear before the near-freezing draft down here cut off the blood supply to his fingers.

A flash of recognition as he looked into the reflection's glazed eyes. Desperation. *Get out.*

He surged back toward the door and grabbed for the handle, eyes on the window and peering into the dark beyond. He squinted, hesitant to open the door without knowing what was out there; what if it was *them*? What if they caught him out there and threw him straight back into the basement?

Worse: what if it was locked? After all, why *wouldn't* it be?

Unable to make sense of any of the dark shapes beyond the glass, the young man drew in a sharp breath and wrenched the handle.

The door swung open with a squeal and he winced, glancing behind him before looking into the dark. Very briefly he registered the tiny wet slap of something slopping over the concrete, somewhere in the basement, then he elected to ignore the sound and focused.

Before him, a narrow, round tunnel yawned into a titanic black hole. He caught a glimpse of steel and discerned a steep, rickety staircase along one tunnel wall. Swallowing, he stepped through the door.

And froze.

The staircase rattled as something emerged from the dark.

8

The boy's heart stopped beating in his chest as terror consumed him and he watched the creature step forward, clutching its belly with both hands, its eyes glinting like tiny silver discs in the shadows. It was breathing heavily, its body bony and hunched over, bare feet padding through puddles of sludge on the concrete.

It hadn't seen him, he realised, taking a step back and watching the creature round the staircase and start to climb. It walked like something broken, one shoulder dipped way down, the other angular and loose. Its head fell forward and thick strings of gloop swung from its maw as it stalked up the stairs, breath coming out in ragged gasps.

"Nope," the young man said, backing away through the door and slamming it shut. He wheeled around on the top step and staggered down, back into the basement—

Something exploded in a wet spray of blood and meat as his heel slammed down into it. There was a loud, wet *pop* as his foot went all the way through and the whistle of air escaping a taut container. He looked down, stunned into silence by the sudden slop of heat that spattered his leg. The gluey, tentacled lung-thing had followed him halfway across the basement; a slimy trail of membranous fluid slithered through the shadows behind it, smeared with blood and viscera.

He stood for a moment in the mess and felt bile rising in his throat as gunk dripped down his leg. Then he moaned, a long, visceral moan from somewhere in his stomach, and the sound echoed throughout the basement as he looked from one pile of bones to another, reeling from the sheer amount of parts scattered and heaped around him, suddenly realising – finally, fully, violently – that he had been dragged down here to suffer—

The boy's eyes moved to the third door and he ploughed toward it, dragging sheets of punctured lung across the concrete with him. Halfway across the basement he noticed a clump of white on the wall and, surging toward it, saw with relief that there were four or five gowns hung on a series of crude hooks. Grabbing one of the gowns, he

9

slung it on. The fabric was thin and papery, like hospital attire. There was a name stitched into the breast:

B. Cooper.

His name, he realised, his blood thickening immediately, freezing him still. His name, imprinted on a gown he'd never worn, hanging on the wall of the grotty basement where he'd woken up. Why? Jesus Christ, why was his name on it?

Because *they* wanted him to put it on, he thought.

They knew he'd need it.

They were watching.

2

Brian Cooper was nineteen years old.

He had been, at least, the day they'd pulled him from the Cambridge UL. The day they'd pulled him from his life. And assuming he'd been unconscious down here for a day or two – perhaps it was more, judging by the drilling hunger cramps currently burrowing through his stomach – then he had been gone from above ground for more than the twenty-four hours the police needed before they declared him Missing. That capital M was important; it meant there were people looking for him.

He was confident that his mother would have gone to the police. He normally rang her from campus at the weekend, and she had Josh's number if she needed either of them for anything. As soon as Cooper had missed their Friday night call at 7:00 P.M., she would have called his boyfriend to make sure they were both okay.

It might be Monday morning by now.

His face would be plastered all over campus. Poor Josh would be going out of his mind; Cooper's mother would already have lost hers and was probably, right this second, trying to get the FBI involved. The boy couldn't have said he'd be particularly upset with her; even if she enlisted a SWAT team or some dumpy private investigator from one of her novels, he'd be glad of the company.

Christ, at this point, maybe even his dad would be worried about him.

They would come for him, he thought, steeling himself at the door. They'd find him.

He just had to get above ground before they gave up looking.

The wheel was heavy, and he grunted loudly as he wrestled it with both hands, the disjointed mechanism screaming in protest. Things were starting to come back to him now. He had a paper due on Wednesday (bollocks if that was going to get done now, but if ever there were *extenuating circumstances*, these were them). He and Josh were supposed to be going out Tuesday night with friends – that was, if he'd managed to finish his paper – and next weekend he was heading home to introduce his boyfriend to the infamous Mr Cooper for the very first time. Cooper's mum had met Josh a few times, but his dad was somewhat less… accepting. Still, this was it, the moment Cooper had been preparing for for the last year and a half, the moment that would propel him, definitively, one way or the other: would he and his father be able to repair their relationship? Or sever all ties for good?

And then he'd been taken. Kidnapped?

Why?

And by whom?

Cooper had to pull with both arms to get the door open, and even then it was a struggle, though finally it swung on rusted hinges with a sound like the one he imagined two aeroplanes would make if they crashed together and scraped each other's paintwork to shreds at thirty-thousand feet. A cloying wall of manure-smell wafted through and blossomed into the meaty stench of the basement, the two fusing so that Cooper was forced to hold his breath. Pausing for a moment, his arms and chest aching from the work of getting the door open, he covered his mouth with one hand and peered around the door.

A wide, round tunnel stretched away from him into the dark, the walls drenched in shadow, the floor a slithery mass of black, bubbling tar. Nearest the door, where the faint glow of the fluorescent lamps in

12

the basement just about permeated, he saw long-faded paint marks on the gritty, brown cement of the tunnel wall, marks that might once have been stencilled numbers but were now little more than flaking red reminders of a civilisation that had dumped its shit underground for centuries. Deep, ragged wounds remained in the walls where chunks had been gouged out, exposing raw clots of aggregate and rusted steel piping. The chunks themselves now lay as eroded heaps of detritus, half-submerged, in the fluid membrane of the rank sewage that flowed in a wide, shallow trench along the tunnel floor.

Far ahead, there was a flickering beacon of amber: another bulb, slowly swinging from the ceiling of the tunnel. It was too dim for him to be able to discern how far. He heard gentle splashing, the slopping sound of something crawling worm-like through the sewage down the tunnel, but he could not see anything. Rats, probably.

Or something else the size of a rat, he thought, thinking of the awful lung-thing he'd stamped into a red spatter.

Cooper shuddered, turning back to the basement and closing his eyes for a moment. He pinched the bridge of his nose, the tension between his eyes enough to draw his focus forward, to the present, to the crux of whatever mess he was in.

He had to go *somewhere*.

But somebody had brought him down here. Somebody had known that he would wake up, and left three – at *least* three – separate exits for him, unguarded, unlocked. That meant that this *somebody* wanted him to leave the basement; they *wanted* him to play along, to engage with whatever sick game this was. He couldn't go up the ladder and through the hatch, not knowing that someone – or something – else had gone that way only moments before he'd woken up. He couldn't go through the other door, because the *thing* he'd seen… well, he was fairly confident that if he went that way, it would see him back.

That left him two options: stay in the basement; or head into the dark, down what looked for all the world like an abandoned sewage system.

Only half-*abandoned*, the groggy voice of his brain provided, *there's a light down there – somebody's still using these tunnels.*

Cooper's eyes snapped open and he looked around the basement one more time. Dark spots of blood bloomed on the walls, specks of long-dried viscera spattering the concrete. Heaps of bone and skin glistened wetly in the half-light. He couldn't stay here.

Perhaps they'd find him in the tunnels, but they'd come to the basement first.

For a long time he stared at the nearest pile of fractured bone, transfixed by it. About four foot high, the mound lay against the wall in an inky spill of shadow, sharp ivory-white pieces of rib and knuckle poking out of the otherwise-shapeless mass. A small mountain of death, fragments of skull laying among scraps of skin and punctured liver. Somewhere near the bottom of the mound, he saw toes poking out and wondered how much of a foot – or leg – they were attached to.

There was something odd about the structure, he realised, gazing deep into the hollow, black pits of a broken skull's eye-sockets. Something not quite right – discounting the obvious.

After a while, he put his finger on it.

The pile was moving.

Only slightly, as though there were insects scuttling among the heap, crawling beneath rotted flaps of skin and tissue and rolling through the rutted canes of a smashed ribcage. Gently the mound shifted, bones slowly grinding against each other, blood trickling down to the concrete floor as it ran through the softly-heaving mass. It was like an odd, hypnotic illusion, like one of those pictures that starts to swirl into a vortex if you look for too long. But this was real.

Something among the bones was moving, and as he watched, it began to move faster. More violently, until it looked like the bones themselves were waking up.

"You need to find something to eat," Cooper murmured to himself, and he turned back to the open doorway and stepped out into the tunnel.

14

3

Cooper heaved the door closed behind him and lay panting against it for a moment, his eyes adjusting to the dark pitch of the tunnel. The tiny beacon of orange up ahead flickered and he was briefly terrified that it would go out completely and leave him in the dark, but thankfully it remained, giving him something at least to head toward.

Eventually he steeled himself, straightened up, and stepped away from the door.

A few feet away the concrete sloped down gently, dropping into the shallow trench of sewage that bubbled softly down the tunnel. Clumps of black that looked like glistening wet knots of seaweed lay in thin rivulets in the stone. Cooper brushed down the thin, ill-fitting hospital gown with both hands, as though removing any dust from it would cleanse him of the stinking filth he found himself suddenly forced to wade through. With a deep breath (one he quickly regretted), he stepped forward.

The stench was cloying and viscous, though thankfully it was largely urine that he could smell. He was sure that there was more mixed into the inches-deep river he was about to walk through, but for now at least he could pretend that it was *only* piss.

That was, until his toes dipped into it.

"Eugh," Brian moaned as the pads of his toes squelched into a half-solid mass of something surprisingly cold. Mud, he thought, pretend it's mud and you'll be just fine. Immediately the invasion of half his foot into the sewage caused a mild ripple and a small surge of dark, bubbling swill trickled up the ramp to caress his heel. He retched.

Behind him, something in the basement fell away from the wall with a soft *thwump* and a rattle of rolling bone. The sound was muffled through the door but he knew that if he, in his weakened state, could open that door then so could anything else. He wasn't safe until he was above ground again. Without stopping to think, he stepped down the ramp and into the sewage.

Ankle-deep in the boggy mess, he slogged forward a few paces before the ripe stench overcame him again and he turned, vomiting into the river. His stomach heaved up all it could but the stream that trickled over his lip was thin and watery. Immediately his gut rumbled, wrenching itself into knots. How long could somebody his age and size survive without food? He could do the maths fairly easily: the amount of time he'd already been down here, plus a few hours at best.

He was going to die.

Something swum quickly away from him as he slogged onward and he watched a fat, bloated lump of something dark and wet slither into the shadows. He'd been right about the rats, then. Moving carefully, he padded slowly through the sewage and kept his eyes on the softly-swinging lightbulb up ahead. It could only have been a couple hundred yards away, a quarter-mile at most. He could manage that, no matter how many rats nipped at his feet.

Greywater swilled about his ankles as he pressed on, toes sinking into a soft, shifting carpet of filth beneath the filmy surface. The pad of his foot stung where urine had seeped into the tiny fresh wound there; there was no way that wouldn't be infected, but that wasn't his priority right now. If he had to amputate his foot, so be it. Christ, he'd give both legs to get out of here.

He was about halfway to the light when something warm and slippery slopped over his foot.

Cooper froze, eyes dropping to the sewage as the thing slipped over his toes and drifted wetly away. He had felt it throb, knew that it was alive, but… it was entirely smooth, not hairy like a rat ought to be. He hadn't felt any legs. It hadn't bitten him.

A few moments passed and the thing didn't resurface, so Cooper pressed on. He had only been walking for a couple minutes; he couldn't stop at every sound or movement, or he'd never get anywhere. He looked around as he walked, squinting into the dark. Occasionally iron rungs poked out of the walls, but there were no hatches or doorways, and many of those rungs were broken and sharp. Every now and then a spider scuttled out of a crack in the wall or a trailing clump of thick nettle fluttered in a breeze coming from somewhere down the tunnel: a sign, at least, that he was going the right way.

Something butted into his ankle and bobbed away. The same smooth, slippery thing that had slid over his foot. Immediately Cooper wheeled around, lashing forward and plunging his hand into the sewage. It splashed his face as he fished for the object, gritting his teeth. His fingers brushed something warm and round and he grabbed for it, scooping it out of the water in an explosion of ice-cold filth. "Hah!" he yelled, squeezing the thing as it wriggled wetly in his hand.

His triumph turned quickly to repulsion and he moaned.

"Oh, what the *fuck*…"

It was a kidney. About twice the size of his hand and a gruesome, dark red, it was fat and sickly and bruised black about its underside. He held the bean-shaped thing for a second, staring blankly at it – and then it *twitched*.

"Yagh!" he yelped, flinging the thing hard at the nearest wall. The kidney smacked concrete with a hollow, wet boom and slid down to the floor, where it swayed for a moment before flopping, finally, back into

17

the sewage. Cooper wiped his hand on his hospital gown, smearing a brown-red comma into the material. Swallowing nervously, he turned and kept walking.

Behind him, something slopped loudly in the water.

Cooper turned back to see a shape swimming toward him, a thin foamy wake streaking past it. Stumbling back, he swung an arm down and grabbed for the thing, which quickly slipped out of his grip and slipped around his heel. Before he could lift his foot out of the water the thing had clamped onto the back of his calf and he watched, incredulous, as the kidney he had thrown into the wall suctioned itself to him and started to coil around his leg. "What the—"

Cooper brought his knee up and swung his leg, trying to shake the thing loose. The kidney clung to him, the skin where it was attached suddenly tingling and numb, and he heard a horrible squelching sound like water being squeezed from a sponge. Tiny white bubbles foamed from the surface of the kidney and thin strings of bloody water swung down into the sewage.

"Get the fuck off!" Cooper yelled, balling his hand into a fist and lunging down, batting the thing off his leg. It came loose with a wet sucking sound and flopped into the water. Quickly he scooped it out and threw it into the wall again, slogging toward it before it could slide back down beneath the surface. "You fuck off, you weird little slimy shit!"

His knuckles plunged into the kidney and smashed into the concrete beneath and he yowled in pain as the wet, wriggling thing burst, rupturing like a water balloon and spraying the wall – and his bare legs – with purple ichor.

"Jesus!" he yelled, stumbling back. "Jesus, fuck, fucking Jesus fucking Christ *fuck*!"

His heart pounded in his ears and he had to stop to catch his breath, his entire body trembling with the mania pumping through him. First that deformed lung-thing, and now this?

"What the fuck is going on?" he yelled, his voice echoing in the tunnel. It boomed back at him and he glanced back toward the basement door, briefly considering heading back that way and waiting in there until they came for him. He had never seen the men that had come for him in the library – they were too fast – but he pictured a group of thick-set thugs in riot gear, military types with guns. Well, let them fucking shoot him, then.

He'd rather that, than… whatever this was.

"No," he muttered, thinking about his mum. About Josh. He had to get away, get above ground, get back to them. No matter how many writhing kidney-things he had to punch. No matter how much shit he had to wade through.

Grinding his teeth together, Cooper turned his head toward the swinging amber light and braced himself. His hands clenched into fists, his stomach knotting into a hungry ball of anguish.

He pressed on.

4

Trudging through the grime became more of a chore as it chilled his feet, the cold swill seeping into his pores and stiffening his legs as he waded. As he reached the first bulb he paused, looking about him, but there were no distinguishing features to mark this section of tunnel, save for the softly-swaying bulb itself and the frayed black cable from which it hung. The greasy glass was smeared with grit and moths buzzed about it, batting their bodies into the bulb with a senseless and repugnant abandon. As he had neared the light Cooper had noticed more and more flies, some trapped in the oily film that coated the surface of the greywater, some hovering loudly above it and poking at splashes of dark colour on the walls.

Nothing to do, he thought, but continue down the tunnel. Ahead, perhaps another quarter mile from the first bulb, he saw a second. Eventually there would be a door, another ladder. Had to be. Didn't matter if he passed ten bulbs or a hundred, he would find one eventually.

He kept walking, stomach growling as the cold piss and shit around his heels gently spattered his calves. Every now and then something small slopped into the sewage nearby and he froze, waited for it to pass, then moved on again.

Just after the third lightbulb, the tunnel began to curve around to the left. He followed the faint glow of a distant fourth bulb, pressing one hand to the wall to steady himself. His nails scratched the concrete as he moved, the rough stone softly grinding down the pads of his fingers. He could only have walked for a mile at most, and hadn't pushed himself to more than walking pace, but his legs ached. He felt dizzy, like he had never moved this far or this fast in his life.

In the faint, flickering glare of the next bulb, he saw life.

He stopped a little way from the hanging thing, letting the swaying halo of light pulse across his face. Beneath the bulb, a lumpen mass of tissue lay festering in the sewage: a translucent, shining coil of intestine snaked through a clump of bulbous, onion-like organs that he couldn't name, all of them fused to a curved panel of bone and cartilage that looked like a hip. Blood had congealed in a globby spray about the edges of the awful shape.

Fungus bloomed from the carnage, colourful splashes of green and orange forming mottled petals around a central pillar of pulsing, blue inkcap. A pair of rats nibbled hungrily at the meat of the deformed shape, their tails thrashing happily in the shallow water as they ate. Flies buzzed around a cacophony of smaller, brightly-coloured mushrooms, each one a plump, dry bud sprouting from the network of crackling electric mycelium that coated the intestines.

When the thing didn't move, Cooper stepped cautiously around it – ignoring the anguished squeals of the rats – and pressed forward. Shuddering from the sight of the awful organic display, he staggered through sewage to the next bulb – how many was that now, six? Seven? – and groaned in disgust. Small clumps of flesh floated on the surface, bobbing gently as he passed. The water was becoming deeper, had been for a few dozen feet, the tunnel sloping lightly downward so that before too long it was halfway to his knees. His legs were frozen and his whole body shivered, and the sewage was thick enough here that it was near-impossible to lift his feet out for every step, so he simply shuffled wetly onward. Shit shifted in thick, silty clouds around his legs as the oily surface broke around him, thick cracks opening in the viscous, hardened scum with every movement he made.

Behind him, something went *schlo—oppp*. There was a small surge at his feet as the swill rippled.

Slowly, he turned his head to look back.

Beneath the last bulb, the little mound of shining organs and pulsing, well-fed fungus lay moveless, silent. Faint ripples spread around it, as if it had turned a little in the swell. Fuck, he thought, had it moved?

For a moment he stared – then there was a skittering sound at the edge of the tunnel and his eyes darted to it. Two rats slipped out of the water and climbed the wall, claws punching into the concrete as they chirped at each other.

"Thank fucking Christ," Cooper breathed, turning back around.

An ice-cold wall of liquid shit smashed into him as something lurched up out of the water, a bubbling rage of shining wet meat launching itself into his stomach. Cooper grunted as the air was punched violently out of his chest, staggering back a pace and grabbing for the thing that had crashed up out of the sewage. Thrusting both hands into the wriggling, wet mass clamping itself to his gut he wrenched it away from him, yelling out as his fingers sunk into something that felt like jelly wrapped in pigskin.

"What the fuck?!" he screamed as the thing lashed about in his hands. "What the fucking fuck is this?!"

He stumbled as the thing writhed and convulsed, latching onto his fingers and hands with gluey flaps of tissue. He spun around, trying to shake it off, to throw it away, but now it was attached, suckering itself to his wrists.

"*What the fuck is happening?!*"

The thing was about half his size, though surprisingly light. Half of a broken ribcage was wrapped protectively around a bloated, throbbing lung and a cauliflower-like blob of tissue that spiralled around lumps of cartilage and thick, meaty chunks of back. The ruptured plate of a single shoulder blade had slid between two halves of what looked like a rotting, black liver, and though the liver had mostly reformed around the invading bone, a sliver of ivory-white poked out like the blade of a kitchen knife. Thick, glistening tubes – like bulging veins, dark red and slippery – exploded from panels of skin and organ, slithering around his wrists like thin tendrils, spurting gobs of pus and blood as they did.

"Get the fuck *off*!" Cooper yelled, staggering toward the nearest wall and smashing both his hands against the concrete. The thing's grip loosened and he took the opportunity to swing his whole body a hundred-eighty degrees, flinging it into the opposite wall. As it hit stone there was a spray of red but the thing remained largely intact, sliding down the wall and back into the sewage. Cooper cried out as it wriggled loudly toward him, splashing gobs of shit onto the walls. Not swimming, he realised dumbly, but *rolling* – digging its broken ribs into the concrete like fingers and then propelling itself forward over the resulting fulcrum, again and again, spilling about like mad—

Cooper yanked his leg back as the thing's tube-tentacles snapped at his calf. Red sparks flashed in his vision as he yelled, launching his fist down into the abomination's centre of mass and grabbing. His fingers thrust deep into something squishy and wet, like cottage cheese, and he ripped his arm back.

Panting, he staggered back, a clump of cauliflower-shaped tissue still wriggling in his hand. The insane organ-creature seemed to recoil momentarily before recentring itself and coming toward him again. Panicking and breathless, Cooper threw the cauliflower into the nearest wall and punched again. Fractured ribs grazed his wrist as his knuckles smashed into the bloated lung, and there was a shrill wheeze as it burst. Blind with anger and confusion, he reached down into the water with both hands and grabbed the thing by the clumped knots of its ribcage, gathering all his strength and ripping his arms out in either direction.

There was a sound like tearing paper and a wet, sickening crunch of bone as the thing ruptured, right down the middle. The tube-tentacles snapped back in pain and the creature fell into the water, two halves flying apart from each other in a spray of blood and fluid.

Blood pumping hotly around his body, Cooper stood in the mess for a minute and gathered his breath.

He blinked in surprise when the shining mass of tissue and fungus beneath the lightbulb started to move.

"Oh, shit," he said, watching in horror as the flies hovering around the thing exploded outward, their little black cloud becoming a murmuration then separating into atoms. The sewage spilled forward as the clump of multicoloured matter rolled over itself, moving slowly as if suddenly awoken.

Cooper looked down into his hand, saw that he was still gripping a clump of broken ribcage. His fingers slipped between the ribs and he held it like a weapon, a four-pronged dagger that curved viciously out of his wrist. Gritting his teeth, he tightened his grip on the ribs and looked up.

The thing surged out of the water toward him, a mass of mushroom and intestine screaming through the dark, glistening shit-spray and streaking the walls with red. "Get fucked!" Cooper yelled, launching his fist forward.

Four curved spears of ribcage plunged deep into the thing, severing a knot of translucent intestine and puncturing two of the weird onion-shaped organs into glittering pulp. Before the thing could fall to the ground Cooper swung his arm to the side, shearing muscle and tissue with the ragged edges of the ribs and cutting the thing clean in two. Quivering mushroom caps fell into the water as chunks of viscera splashed the wall.

Chest heaving, Cooper staggered back, the bloody piece of ribcage tumbling from his hand and plopping into the water.

Turning quickly, he slopped through the mess of the things that had attacked him and continued down the tunnel, knowing that if he stopped he'd throw up again, and he didn't have enough left in him for that. He had to get out of here. Fast.

Staggering past the next lightbulb, he looked desperately around for another and saw it off to the right, the tunnel curving away again.

24

Clumsily he rushed around the corner, blinking into the dark. A tiny spot of amber up ahead, winking in and out of existence as it flickered weakly.

Knee-high in waste now, he waded through chunks of bone and deflated organ, more and more of them bobbing in the water the further he went down the tunnel. Gunk dripped from the ceiling and flies hovered over the scum in a thick cloud of chitinous black. The stink was unbearable.

"Ladder," he moaned to himself over and over, looking all around for some way out, "ladder, must be a ladder…"

A big, dark shape floated in the water before him and he scanned the surrounding sludge with his eyes, wondering if there was enough space to pass before it woke up. Or perhaps he'd missed something, back the way he'd come – a side tunnel, or an opening in a dark spot—

Before he could plan his next move the thing moved, rearing out of the water in an ugly spray of red.

Cooper's heart skipped a few beats and he felt bile rising into his mouth.

"*He—eelp…*" the thing whispered, and Cooper vomited for the third time.

5

The only way to describe it would have been to say that it was about thirty-to-forty per cent of a human.

The thing swayed before him, half-in and half-out of the water, sewage and blood dripping off it and glistening in the dim light. It had a decent amount of torso, two slabs of striated muscle forming a crude, half-knitted chest, stringy knots of back-flesh wound around a stiff, unpolished section of spine. Its left arm was nothing but a wiry stump, a mess of gently oozing cables at its shoulder, but the right was nearly complete, and it used this to prop itself up.

The half-finished muscles of its shoulder knotted up into a bloated, white neck and this became a grinning jaw, teeth flashing in a gummy, raw clamp of tissue that wriggled on loose hinges as it spoke. There was no face – it had no eyes or head, no brain to speak of – but the ragged jaw gnashed together of its own volition, a soft, slopping voice escaping between putrid slug-like lips:

"*He—eelp… you?*"

Cooper was frozen stiff. The thing's head was gone – at least, the top two-thirds of it – but he couldn't shake the feeling that the creature was staring into his soul. It stood awkwardly on its single hand, the meaty folds of its back propping up its back end, and wobbled slowly in the water.

"*Help you?*"

"You…" Cooper whispered, dumbfounded. "You want to help me? What the fuck are you?"

The creature grinned. That seemed to be its default setting. Teeth grinding together, it said, "*Way out… is through. Need… my he—eelp.*"

"I reckon I'm doing okay so far," Cooper said, bunching his fists together.

The thing swayed before him, dark slugs of blood dribbling over its wriggling lower jaw. "*Worse… to come. Need help. Hungry…*"

As if on cue, Cooper's stomach rumbled again.

"*Tell you… which meat is good.*"

Cooper swallowed. Said nothing, cautiously shaking his head.

"*Which meat is bad.*"

Slowly, he turned to look behind him.

Lying in a rippling mess of cold shit, a blood-red gaggle of spattered organs lay still among the clumps of meat that had held them together. Ripped coils of intestine twitched gently.

"*Hung—*"

"Yeah, no," Cooper said, turning back to the creature. "I think I'm good."

I'm going insane.

"Now, if you don't mind…"

He slogged past the creature, taking as wide a berth as possible. There was a sound like recently-caught salmon struggling in a bucket of ice as it turned its half-head toward him. "*Worse… to… come…*"

Cooper paused. Closed his eyes.

I've gone *insane.*

"Leave me the fuck alone, you weird cunt," he said quietly, and he walked on down the tunnel.

6

Cooper had rounded another bend when he felt a faint ripple in the water.

It was up past his knees now, almost at his waist, and he knew that this meant the tunnel was sloping deeper, that he was heading farther underground with every step. But he couldn't go back now, even if he thought that returning to the basement and trying to leave via the ladder was suddenly a good idea – he could hear more of the dreadful organ-things sloshing slowly about in the tunnel behind him and knew that he was being followed, that if he turned around he'd have to face more of them than before. No, if he kept going there would be a way out somewhere. There had to be.

A sudden bolt of hunger ripped through his stomach and he bent over double, groaning with the pain. It was searing, a bright spark of absolute emptiness that struck the base of his chest and spilled right down to his feet, making his legs weak and his whole body convulse. Black clouds pooled into his vision, seeping like fog. His head pounded.

He staggered forward, both hands on his belly, forcing himself to keep going. The stench of rotten meatstuff and thick, putrid ranks of turd made the thought of eating unbearable, but he knew he had to find something soon. Somehow.

Rounding a corner, Cooper slogged clumsily through the greywater and looked ahead to the next lightbulb. They were getting further and further apart, he thought, or perhaps he was just becoming quickly weaker as he waded through the bog. Hunger tearing at him, digging its thick claws into his stomach and twisting, he pressed forward.

He had walked for almost another mile when he found it.

Halfway up the wall, a gently, pulsing ball of opaque, purplish tissue clung to the concrete. It was about twice the size of his fist and sagged awfully, a sac of bloated and mucus-covered colour filled with something solid and throbbing. He couldn't have begun to guess what kind of organ this was. That was a good thing. It didn't bear thinking about.

Slowly, he approached. Swallowed nervously.

The thing grew excited as he came near, quivering all over. Its pulsing movements quickened, like the hungry breathing of a pervert leering over their next victim. Or the rapid heartbeat of something depraved upon seeing a masterpiece of the gore and destruction that gave it pleasure.

It sickened him.

Cooper flexed his fingers, standing by the thing and taking in a deep breath. The stink of meat filled his throat and he coughed, immediately regretful. This was a mistake. God, dear fuck, this was a mistake.

Reluctantly, he reached toward the pulsing sac with both hands and thrust his fingernails into the meat.

He balked. It was slippery, his nails piercing a thin membrane which snapped open audibly then sliding into something that felt like warm, raw chicken. Soft and squishy.

It's the only thing down here that isn't covered in shit, he reminded himself. And this, at least, was true: if the slack-jawed creature had told him that there was good meat down here, as well as bad, then it must have meant the type that he didn't have to fish through sewage for. Could it get any better than that, down here?

Repulsed, Cooper ripped open the sac and fumbled to catch the ball of solid, squirming tissue that slipped out of it. He looked up to the ceiling, refusing to lay eyes on the thing in his hand, and gingerly opened his mouth.

He shoved it inside, all in one, instantly gagging as the thing wriggled and writhed against the roof of his mouth. Holding his breath, he clamped down his teeth and a sudden burst of hot, wet fluid splashed the back of his throat as the thing popped between his incisors. Refusing to chew any more than he had to, Cooper swallowed desperately, again and again, sloughing awful greasy chunks of organ down into his throat.

"Oh god," he moaned, laying a hand on his stomach and doubling over again as the acrid taste filled his throat. Was this better than the hunger? He fancied he could feel it inside him, still wriggling, still warm, as it slid down into his digestive system. "Oh god, why would you—"

He threw up, his stomach reacting violently to the sudden invasion and squeezing hard. Wet chunks splashed his chest and he groaned, looking down to see bits of yellow and white swilling in the folds of the fabric.

Well, at least he hadn't vomited *all* of it.

Cooper walked a little farther, sticking to one side of the trench, wading past chunks of tissue in the swell that foamed and gently rippled around him.

In the faint glow of a greasy bulb half a mile down the tunnel Cooper stopped, letting the water still around him. He was cold to the bone, terrified by the small chunks of flesh and viscera that bobbed in the sewage nearby.

Slowly, he turned his head.

He waited, listening for the sounds of movement. All he could hear was the faint dripping of sewage from the ceiling and the distant movements of creatures in the tunnel behind him. Not close enough to concern him.

But he was sure something had moved…

Satisfied that he was alone, Cooper pressed on, swinging his whole body to wade through the greywater. It splashed his chest and arms as he moved, the borrowed hospital gown floating around his waist and exposing his genitals to the filth. When this was done, he thought, he would shower for a week. Fuck the paper that was due in – and any more deadlines to come – he was quitting university and moving to Iceland, where he could spend the rest of his life sitting in a hot spring. Josh could come too. That might be nice. He wondered if they'd start to argue, if they spent the rest of their lives together. If they'd start to turn into his parents. Surely not every relationship ended up like that… right? He was only nineteen. They had time to make their own path. Their own lives.

Unless I die down here.

A warm stream of bubbles passed between his legs and he froze still, eyes flitting down to the surface. Something behind him. Right behind him…

Again, he turned.

For a moment there was nothing. The surface of the water was completely still, save for dribbles of foam where the crumbling stone walls had eroded into the slurry. Even the dripping seemed to have stopped.

Then he saw it. A dark, slender shape beneath the surface, snaking slowly toward him.

Cooper's mouth opened, but nothing came. The thing moved like an eel, but it was longer than that, much longer: tracking its slim, snake-like body with his eyes he couldn't see a tail, or an end; it seemed to curve right around the corner and keep going.

Suddenly it thrashed out of the water and launched itself at him, little more than a streak of cauliflower-white and a splash of blood. There was a piercing shriek as it snapped viciously at his chest and Cooper ducked to one side, the thing narrowly missing him—

Before he could move completely out of the way it had snapped back, cracking like a whip as it lashed around his waist. It slapped his flesh hard, a length of wet, squishy rope smacking his spine as it coiled quickly around him. Then it was slithering down his leg, squelching loudly as it curled around his calf and tightened. "Get off!" he yelled, struggling to move as folds of the great long thing surged out of the water and snapped around his free leg, squeezing his thigh as they coiled tighter, tighter, tighter. It was an intestine, he realised sickly, coated in shit and mucus and impossibly long – he vaguely remembered something about a small intestine being stretched out to cover an entire tennis court – surely it couldn't be that long…

He didn't have a chance to react, or to try and pull the thing off him; before he could blink or scream another twitching length of intestine had constricted his chest and stomach, winding itself around him again and again, cutting off the air to his lungs, squeezing it out of him. More coils snapped around his arms and wrists, yanking him down toward the surface of the water. His eyes bulged as something lashed his neck, squeezing his throat, slipping wetly into his mouth and pressing down his tongue.

He gagged as bulging folds of warm, convulsing tissue forced their way into his throat, lashing lengths of it strangling the blood supply to his arms and legs, dragging him down to his knees and pulling him to the water. It meant to drown him, he realised breathlessly, choke him out or drown him, whichever came first—

There was a sound like elastic stretching too far, and something warm and wet splashed his face.

Cooper looked up as the intestine's grip on his chest and throat started to loosen. His eyes widened as he saw an enormous shadow lurch across the tunnel wall and he watched helplessly as the shape thrust its head forward to bite, teeth gnashing in the dark.

The intestine-creature screeched, withdrawing so suddenly from inside his mouth that he thought it had dragged half his windpipe out with it. He gasped for air and instantly sucked in a revolting stream of mucus, his breathless moan turning to a wet, hacking cough.

In horror, he watched as the one-armed creature with the muscular slabs for a chest and just a ragged jaw where its head should have been rounded the corner into sight, leering down to bite savagely. It had already severed the intestine in several places and separate lengths of white, spongy organ wriggled around it as a thick, clotted red mist spread and seeped into the water.

The intestine – what was left of it – finally retreated into the water and freed his legs as the creature clamped its teeth down hard and ripped another chunk out with a spray of gore and internal fluids. Cooper fell back against the wall, panting as he clutched for his throat and tried to regain his breath. "Jesus… fuck… what the fucking *fuck*…"

The creature looked at him – looked at him with its mouth – and smiled thinly, fleshy strings of intestine hanging over its lower jaw. "*Need… help?*" it rasped.

Cooper nodded. "Sure," he breathed. "Why the hell not?"

7

The one-armed thing dragged itself through the sewage, gargling oily streaks of brown as its lower jaw filtered the surface of the water. Cooper followed reluctantly, his arms and legs sore, bruises already forming under the skin.

"You saved my life," he said quietly as they passed a rusted iron grille in the wall. They had passed a couple of these now: once tunnel openings that led further into the labyrinth, now they were barred off and impossible to pass through. They had no choice but to keep following the main path. "Why did you do that?"

"*Help... you...*" the thing said, bubbles slipping through the grimy filters of its jaw as it opened and shut, "*help... me...*"

"So you help me get out of here," Cooper said, "and then I help you... what?"

The creature dragged itself forward, slopping awfully through the mire, and echoed: "*Help you... help me.*"

"You want to get out of here too, huh?"

"*Out. Up.*"

"Sounds good. So we just keep going?"

"*Up ahead... danger.*"

"Is there another way?" Cooper asked nervously.

Slowly the creature turned, pivoting on the arm buried in sewage. Behind it, strips of back-flesh floated on the surface around the slivers of bone and cartilage that poked up from beneath the murky water. Gently, it tilted its jaw, the smashed teeth and bones slithering over a bloated white tongue. It was looking behind him, Cooper realised. Pointing, in the only way it could. He looked over his shoulder and swallowed.

Behind them, shapes floated slowly forward in the dark. Shining orbs of tissue bobbed on the water as clumps of flesh and sponge, fused together and clamped to shanks of bone like leeches, swum using their severed tendons and veins as paddles. Looking up, he saw more of the things crawling forward on the walls, flattened pancake-like slabs of purplish liver and stomach suctioned to the concrete and flopping over themselves in a gelatinous, arduous squabble to get to him.

"I guess that's a no, then," Cooper said.

He followed the creature, hurrying now. His face and chest were covered in sludge and the flies had started to clot the air around him, hovering about the stained gown he wore and harassing the material. Midges buzzed in his face and, though he knew not to wave them away, he thought he might very well give in to temptation at any moment. He was confused. Terrified. Hungry. And he was pissed off, at this point, no longer moving through a haze of incredulity but alert to the fact that something was entirely wrong down here, and that someone – somewhere – had forced him into this situation.

He groaned, clutching at his stomach as a deep pang of hunger cut through him. it was like a scythe in his gut, slowly turning, cropping the flesh of his insides until there was nothing left. A hollow pit with sharp edges and nothing but longing within.

He needed to eat again.

What the hell were these things? They all looked human – from what he knew of anatomy, at least, though the last time he'd seen even a diagram of the digestive system had been in college – but they seemed to have some weird, twisted sentience that he couldn't comprehend.

35

Organs and pieces of bone didn't have brains, for one thing, so how could they think? They shouldn't have been able to move, or attack him like that, and now they all seemed *driven* to do so, like they had some screwed-up purpose… how was any of this possible? And why were they all so… fucked? Why were they all knitted-up together like that?

And where the fuck was he?

And why the fuck?

And, again, *what* the fuck?

And—

"Fuck."

They had rounded a bend in the tunnel. Cooper stopped dead, ignoring the distant splashing sounds behind him. He stared in horror.

"*Up ahead…*" the slack-jawed creature rasped.

"Yeah," Cooper said bluntly. "Danger. I get it."

The tunnel stretched out before them for about three-hundred yards, a prehistoric hollow of concrete drilling straight forward into the dark. Here the sewage bubbled and dark phantoms of shadow shifted wraith-like over the walls as a single, dead bulb swung from the ceiling.

Right down the end of the tunnel, swamped in oozing swathes of darkness, a narrow ladder was riveted to the wall. Gritty iron rungs stamped into the concrete led up to a round, metal hatch in the ceiling, the size of a manhole cover: rusted at the edges so that it looked as if it had been scorched with fire and sprayed with copper shavings. Escape.

Between them and it, the tunnel was awash with remains. A grim, gory explosion of red and purple had painted the walls, the ceiling. The slurry of sewage around it was filled with oily, swirling pools of blood and pus and seeping white organ-juice. Between Cooper and the way out was a long, spongy cavern of stomach and skin, great heaps of organic matter strewn about and heaving, shuddering as the individual lumps of tissue and long, bloated strips of liver and bladder and bright yellow meat slopped and sludged over each other. Chunks of bone and deformed, half-fused pieces of foot and hip rolled about in the mess, long tendrils of nervous matter sprawling and spreading among it all.

There was not an inch of concrete uncovered; even the waist-high greywater was piled so high with heaps of discarded, throbbing *stuff* that a great island of intestine and blood had spread and become a land mass, a pulsing, breathing mass that he'd have to wade through if he had any hopes of getting out of here.

Cooper gritted his teeth, balling his hands into his fists.

Beside him, the slack-jawed creature appeared to tense, at least in those parts of its half-formed body where such a thing was possible, seemingly preparing to bite and gnaw its way through the horror.

"Ready?" Cooper said quietly.

"*Help... you,*" Slackjaw rasped, "*help* me."

"I'll take that as a yes, then," Cooper smiled weakly, and they moved forward.

8

The mass of organ and tissue seemed to awaken as they came closer, reacting to the gentle swilling of sewage by heaving as one, every lump and strip of fleshy gore quivering excitedly. Cooper swallowed, his eyes flitting from wet chunks of bone to wriggling spirals of intestine, and he noticed that there were other, more recognisable parts in the mix too: here and there eyeballs had been scattered, some glued shut and some burst into little pools of white jelly. Those that were intact and open were focused on him and twitched in unison as he moved. He spotted teeth sprayed about one section of the grim organic island like pebbles, a clump of deep, throbbing brown-purple where three or four stomachs had fused together into one repulsive mountain.

They were about a dozen feet away from the thing when it started to fling itself at them.

There was a deep wet sucking sound and Cooper yelped as several gobs of organ separated from the main body of mass, screaming through the air with a whistle and the flutter of flapping tube-tendrils. "Fuck!" he yelled, raising both arms to bat the clumps away from his face. He managed to grab one and squeezed hard enough that it burst in his fist, spraying the water and the walls around him. Another suckered itself to his neck and he looked down, saw that it was a wrinkled, pink knob of brain. Quickly he ripped it off his throat and tossed it against the wall, where it exploded into grey-pink sludge and drippled quickly down the concrete.

All at once the sewer was alive with noise, a thunder of sloppy raindrops interrupted by squeals and whistles and awful guttural moans. Tiny black holes opened and blinked shut all over the gigantic mass of flesh as it moved and writhed, each one producing dreadful-smelling vapour and spurts of blood.

Cooper ploughed forward through a rain of tissue, glancing toward the slack-jawed creature to see it swinging its spinal column violently into an attacking femur. The bone flew into a swimming blob of flesh and fat and was immediately sucked inside; Cooper's eyes widened as the bone and fat were knitted together by tendrils of skin and formed a dripping, pinkish hammer-shaped thing. His eyes were torn away from the awful sight as something wet exploded into his face; he ducked another blast of viscera and screamed as he bowled his fist into something that looked like a clump of diaphragm with a scalp and a knot of matted hair fused to it. The thing flew into the water and splashed an advancing section of ribcage.

Yelling, Cooper brought up a knee and slammed it into the pulsing sac of a gunky stomach-heart hybrid. The thing's thin, snake-like tendrils writhed as it shrieked shrilly through a tiny, slit in its ventricle and it smashed into a snake-like coil of intestine which had sprung back to strike. Beside him, Slackjaw had clamped its teeth into a slab of meat with fingers and knuckles that Cooper assumed was some kind of deformed arm. Blood sprayed the ceiling as the fingers scrambled desperately to grab Slackjaw by the throat, then all the movement faded from them as an enormous gush of red filtered through the creature's teeth and spilled down into the greywater.

Together they powered through the onslaught, more and more pieces of the gargantuan organic island separating and flinging themselves into the tunnel. A storm of blood-streaked tissue and organic fabric streaked the tunnel walls red and thick, swilling pools of pus and clear fluid spread quickly into the sewage. The flickering light from the last bulb cast tall, sludgy shadows onto the walls as carnage ripped through the air. Cooper punched and bit, slamming his back into the nearest wall when a gaggle of throbbing kidneys latched to his gown, almost enjoying the burst of wet warmth that came when they exploded. He thrust his hand into a network of nerve endings and veins, ripping and shredding so that the enormous ball of muscle they were attached to deflated with an agonised hiss and retreated into the mire.

Before he knew it he had reached the island, a great unsteady, quivering mess of solid red slop that shuddered and throbbed on the surface of the water. All around him organs bounced off the walls and screamed through the sewage, severed arteries flailing wildly. Somewhere behind him, he heard Slackjaw groan gutturally as it crushed a section of cartilage-inlaid throat with its single hand and bit clean through a length of hardened, twisting skin.

Cooper looked past the island of blood to the ladder and gritted his teeth. Something splatted the ceiling above him and a brief spell of hot, red rain sprayed his face.

Covered in blood and exhausted, Cooper took one powerful, wading stride forward and leapt.

He landed sprawling on the island, hands and elbows sinking into a mucus-covered carpet of stomach lining. Scrambling to his feet, he stumbled awkwardly forward, reminded of a half-deflated bouncy castle – if that bouncy castle was slick with blood and quivering with hunger. Something latched onto his left ankle and he ripped his foot forward, screaming as another knot of tube-tendrils snapped around his right and yanked him down. He grabbed for the ladder – god, it was so close now – and yelled in agony as a wall of thick wet matter slammed into his back and forced him onto his knees. Sinking further into the island-mass he shrieked as it started to envelop him, folding around his body, consuming him, sucking him inside—

Cooper struggled, thrusting both hands into slabs of muscle and ripping, tearing, reaching for something deep in the thing's centre that might kill it. Shit and blood filled his mouth as the island collapsed around him, closing over his throat. *This is it,* he thought, *Jesus Christ, I'm going to fucking die here.*

There was a loud smacking sound behind him and he struggled to turn his head, tendrils suckering to his neck and tyring to pull his head back around. Bewildered, he saw through thick folds of red and pink a faint silhouette coming toward him, burrowing, drilling through the gore.

Slackjaw burst through a hunk of meat in a violent explosion of viscera, savagely biting and clawing at the enormous island-creature as it swung lumps of bone and cartilage into a swirling, sentient vortex of white and pink. Cooper started to struggle harder, mania pumping through him, revitalised by the sight of the awful half-formed creature that had decided to help him. He punched and grabbed, ripped and tore and clamped down his teeth to tear away great chunks of organ, all the while running out of air, suffocating, dying. He propelled himself deeper into the island and grabbed shanks of bone, plunging them deep into sacs of muscle and shearing great holes in the island-thing's fleshy wings, shredding and fighting and forcing until—

Air.

Cooper gasped, sucking in a fresh spout of sewage and immediately coughing it up. He scrambled to his feet, waist-deep in greywater but free of the all-consuming wall of tissue he had sunk into. He wheeled around, his entire body soaked in blood and mucus and stinking, human filth, crude bone knives clutched in both fists, coils of artery knotted into his hair and swinging from his arms. Breathing heavily, he looked back at the island of blood and saw…

Stillness.

It quivered softly, weakly, severed through the middle and ruptured into chunks. What had been a concentrated mass of gore was now spread back through the sewage tunnel, pieces of it sprayed on the walls, more bubbling gently on the surface. Cooper backed away from the mess and his back hit something hard and cold – metal, jutting out of the wall – and he spun around, triumphant, desperately looking up—

The ladder.

He had made it.

He reached gingerly for the nearest rung, suddenly afraid that it might be a trick, or that he wouldn't be able to get the hatch open, that he'd be stuck down here forever.

Before he could take hold of the rung a sudden dark knot of pain sliced through his stomach. The hunger was so intense, so incredible that he crumpled to his knees, both hands clutching at his belly as the knot tightened, pulling his chest into a spasm. He was starving, so hungry he thought he might actually die. After all that shit, he might just die because he'd been down here too long; god, what a fucking nightmare.

"Uungh…" he moaned, squeezing his eyes shut to blot out the dark clouds that swamped his vision. Oh, god. Oh god, it was bad. "No, not now, not like…"

Behind him, something splashed in the water.

Squinting through his lashes, hands still clamped to his stomach, Cooper turned his head.

Slackjaw limped toward him, dragging itself forward on its good hand, several chunks of vertebrae missing from its gory tail. Its jaw was crooked and looser than before, and it was covered with blood.

"*Helped… you…*" Slackjaw whispered, its voice a gravelly husk of what it had been. It tipped its jaws backward, as if looking up toward the hatch. "*Help… me?*"

Cooper nodded. Smiled weakly. "Yeah," he muttered, his own voice hoarse and useless. "Sure."

Then he reached down and grabbed Slackjaw by the spine, yanking his elbow back with all the force he could muster as he ploughed the heel of his free hand into the creature's shoulder. There was a dreadful sucking sound as the thing's spine was ripped right out of it in a spray of red, throat and jaw snapping back as slabs of muscle flopped down limply. Cooper scooped his hand into Slackjaw's striated chest and dragged out a cupful of wriggling, meaty tissue, which he quickly stuffed into his mouth. He ate quickly and desperately, ignoring the smell and the taste, ignoring the creature's panicked twitching, digging for more meat and shoving handfuls of it into his throat.

When he was done, Slackjaw was just twitching tubes and gristle.

Eventually, the creature's remains stilled.

Cooper's stomach rumbled, but he recognised the queasy movements of his gut as those of revulsion, not hunger. The lesser of two evils. Slowly, he stood, wiping his hands on his gown and succeeding only in smearing the blood and shit around. "Thank you," he said to the loose, broken jaw at his feet, floating in a waist-high pool of sewage. "For everything."

Looking up toward the hatch, he grimaced and began to climb.

PART II

A

TOWN

CALLED

PERIL

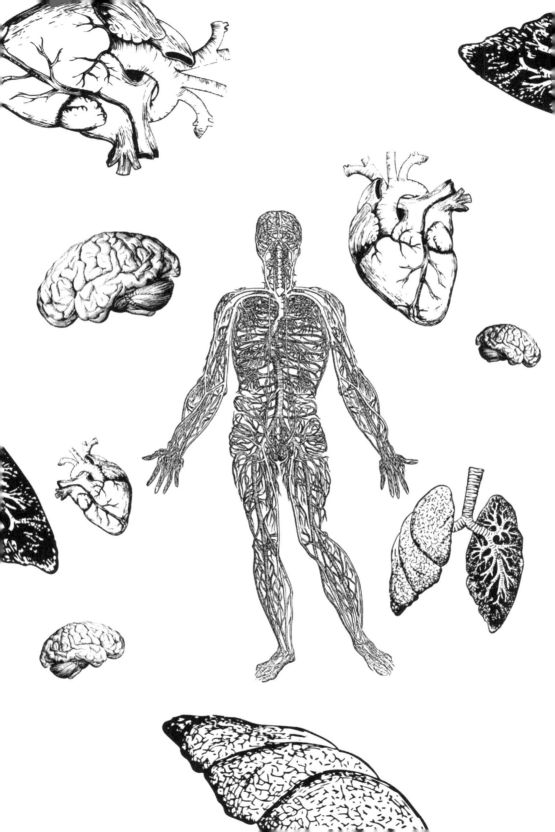

9

Brian Cooper crawled out through the narrow opening and staggered to his feet, weak body sore and aching from the climb. Grimly he shunted the metal drain cover back into place with his heel, cringing at the metallic whine as it shivered into the earth.

Out in the open. Free. The ragged, papery cloth of the hospital gown clung wetly to his back, his legs and arms bare and exposed to a thick biting wind. He stumbled forward a pace, the fleshy soles of his feet picking up a coat of sandy grit as they pressed into the ground. A coarse, dusty cloud of dirt blossomed around his heels as he stood, grateful for the cool dusk air on his face and the light of the waning sun above him. It was soon to set but for now the sky was a clotted swirl of purple and yellow, clouds bleeding with straight banks of luminescence, bright orange fire sweeping the horizon.

Looking around, Brian saw faint smudges in the dust, crooked buildings that looked like they'd been ripped right out of some historical, old-west battleground.

Wooden-slatted walls leaned on stilts and broken porch covers, wide streets of dirt and sand pooling between them in the grim spotlights of a couple dozen old gas streetlamps. He turned a slow circle, eyes shifting from one dilapidated shack to the next, his heart sinking fast. He had hoped he'd come up above ground somewhere close to home, but this was…

Nowhere.

It was like one of those nuclear towns. Big empty husks dressed up to look like minimalist houses, devoid of life and unfurnished – hollow shells that gave the impression of homeliness, erected purely to add some colour to the testing ground before it was blasted to oblivion.

Except it looked like the bomb had already gone off. The earth around him was flat and scorched, the dirt stony and dry where it wasn't cracked into deep, black chasms. The gas lamps gave him the impression that somebody had dumped a bunch of Whitechapel-inspired streets, still drenched with the blood of half a dozen slaughtered prostitutes, into the middle of the desert where they could be forgotten. And he'd been dumped out here with them – not even in the nuclear wild-west dustscape but *beneath* it, where nobody would remember he'd ever existed.

He turned in a slow circle, realising that he'd come up in the middle of what looked like a crude, misshapen village square. A network of streets led away from him, filtering between wooden identikit houses with smashed windows and slanted, sagging rooves. One of the buildings was a little taller and shaped like a wide, sharp-cornered *L*, like a brothel-cum-bar that had gone into ruin. A ramshackle archway between two houses was scratched with carvings of some kind, and beyond it he fancied he could make out a couple of glassy storefronts. The tall, smudged spires of a school building stuck out behind a clump of plain huts to his left.

Twenty or so paces from where he stood, a raised wooden dais lurched out of the sand, a stubby set of steps leading up to a splintery platform. A tall gallows had been erected and a single frayed noose hung from it over a section of the platform that was clearly designed to fall through at the pull of a lever. The noose swung gently in the wind.

Brian was stood right in the middle of some crappy John Wayne movie, but the crew had abandoned the shoot and all the extras had gone home.

Slowly he headed toward the edge of the square, glancing up as he passed the wooden archway erected between the nearest buildings. Words had been clawed into a polished, driftwood plaque nailed to the archway, but most of the letters had faded, smoothed out over the years by the wind, so that all that was left was:

PER / L   IGH STR ET

'High Street' was easy, but the rest… 'Peril'? Was that the name of this place? No, he could make out the faint imprint of the missing letters – maybe an *O* there, and that long-lost scratch might once have been another *E*. It didn't matter.

Wherever he was, he wasn't staying.

He continued toward the larger of the buildings nearest to him, focusing on the large *L*-shaped structure as though discerning its nature might give him a better idea as to where he'd found himself. He was nowhere near home, that was for sure, but if he could just figure out what county he was in – if he could find a map, or a phone, or even something to drink – he would feel much closer to where he needed to be.

He wondered if his mother was still looking for him. At this point he figured the most he could have been gone was a few days, a week maybe. Even if his dad had convinced his mother that he wasn't worth the time and resources, then Josh would still be looking. He could rely on that.

Oh, he missed them. What the hell was he going to tell them when he got back?

If he got back?

Limping slowly through the dust, Brian made it to the porch of the largest building and looked up. There was a faded sign above the closed wing doors, smeared with shades of red and yellow that made the once-gold lettering entirely unreadable. The place stunk of stale liquor and blood, coppery scents filtering out through the doors and onto the cool breeze. Shivering, he heaved himself up onto the porch, a thin splinter immediately sliding into his heel and making him gasp sharply.

The porch stretched across the face of the building, wide windows either side of the door blown inward. Black bin liners had been stapled to the window-frames and billowed softly in the wind, wooden slats boarded over a couple of panes; presumably they had rotted out of the rest, for rusted nails poked out of the wood and bent into vicious iron hooks. The wall itself was a ruin of dry beech and driftwood, the planks a mismatched nightmare of crude pieces and ancient half-assed repairs. There was an old bench beneath each window, but they hadn't been occupied for years.

The wind whistled past him as Brian stepped up to the wing doors and pushed them open. There was an awful scream as the hinges complained; drawing a deep breath, he crossed the threshold into the dark.

A clump of roaches separated and scuttled into a far corner, something larger shifting loudly and lazily among piles of debris at the back of the wide open room in which he found himself. There was no light, but the faint glow of dusk followed him inside, pale beams of grey falling onto the surface of a round, pine table near the door. After a few moments his eyes adjusted to the near-pitch of the rest of the room and he saw that he was, indeed, in an old bar, tables and chairs scattered and bowled over. The floorboards were rotten in places and great black gashes in the floor were surrounded by heaps of dust and sand that had blown in and caked onto the walls. In the centre of the saloon a chair had slipped through a ragged black hole in the floor and half the table had followed, its legs sucked into the sand, rat-shit and old beer stains mottling its surface. Cobwebs were strung from the corners like great misplaced curtains. To his left, a shallow bar counter was piled up with cockroach shells and the bones of dead mice, little wet clumps of fur and meat still clinging to their tiny ribs and skulls. A shiny, oil-black crow feasted on the innards of a recently-deceased rat on top of the only barstool which hadn't fallen over, pinching with its great knife-like beak and sucking wet pinkish knots of tissue from the polished bowl of the rat's punctured head.

"Last call," Brian murmured, thinking back to his first week at university. He had met Josh in the scholars' bar; neither of them particularly liked to drink, but they had been coerced by their respective flatmates into partaking in a freshers' mixer. The smell of whiskey and body odour had been pervasive and rank but he had lasted somehow till gone eleven, having watched many of his new friends disappear leglessly into the bathroom or flop like wet fish into their new homes beneath the bar tables.

"Not a big drinker, eh?" Josh had said, sidling up behind him at the bar and nodding to Brian's glass, still half-full of Guinness.

"Nah," Brian said. "That's my dad. You having a good time?"

"Not really."

Brian had swallowed. Josh had one of the kindest faces he'd ever seen, even scrunched up in mock disgust like that. He had gorgeous dark skin and thick, black hair, little clusters of freckles buried into the shallow dents either side of his nose. His eyes were on fire. Stirred by something that he'd never felt before, Brian did something he didn't know he had the courage to do: he said, "Do you want to?"

As he stepped forward the pad of his left foot crunched a desiccated mouse carcass loudly. Somewhere in the darkness that clung to the saloon walls and obscured the rotten skirting boards from view, a hidden creature chirruped in response.

"Yes," Josh had said, incredibly, and the rest – as they say – was a Bachelor's in History that neither of them would ever use in the real world.

Behind the abandoned bar counter, a white plaster wall stacked with empty shelves was sprayed messily with gobs of something thick and black and congealed. A narrow staircase lilted up into a narrow, black archway behind the wall, many of the stairs worn down and sagging, some missing altogether.

Dismayed by the state of the old bar, Brian stepped around the bar and headed for the stairs. The feeding crow fluffed its wings once as he drew near, then apparently deciding he was too big to bother with, returned to its meal with a loud shucking sound. There was an awful smell behind the bar as though something had died right by his feet, but he ignored it and pushed forward.

Gripping the banister rail, he reeled as his palm found the wood hot and sticky. Withdrawing his arm, he elected to climb without support, moving carefully up past the first missing step and approaching the rest with caution. The stairs groaned as he climbed, each panel of wood screaming violently and unnecessarily.

Rats scarpered as he came onto a narrow landing. At the end of the hall a wooden door was boarded shut, thick slats nailed across it at irregular angles. There was a great chunk of pine missing from the door, ripped out so that he could see into the bathroom beyond, the tiles sprayed with black and grey.

A limp, white shape lay bloated and still in the bathtub, its face ruined by bites and scratches.

Turning to the nearest door, Brian stepped through quickly and found himself in a wide bedroom, the ceiling slanting down toward the head of a grotty double mattress laid directly on the floorboards. The floor was covered with nests of twisted wood and old, wet newspaper and heaps of past were slopped up against the walls and plastered onto the furniture. Somebody had gone insane in this room.

Slowly, ducking as the ceiling lowered above him, Brian moved to the window at the back of the room. There was another behind him, through which he imagined he would see the square and the gallows he had encountered when he came up from underground. For now he was more interested in the rest of the town.

The window was boarded up but the boards were old and chewed up by dust and mould; he grabbed the first and ripped it cleanly off the nails embedded in the frame, the tangy smell of sawdust rising into his nostrils as damp chunks of bright orange wood fluttered away from him. The second took a little more pulling but the third came easily. Quickly he tore away the ragged, moth-eaten bin liner that covered the window and looked outside, gripping the splintery sill with both hands.

The town crawled slowly across the sand beneath him, rooves with gaping black holes lit by the swirling matrix of purple-gold clouds above. A great bank of pressure squeezed the sizzling orange sun into a rubbery mess on the horizon, the last boughs of its light spilling over crooked empty streets and spangling over mounds and blankets of shattered glass. A haze of fog drifted through the beams and banisters of leaning porches, an antediluvian swamp-mist that seeped over the sand and threatened to consume everything. The high street was a jawbone-shaped curve of store fronts; over to his left, an abandoned schoolyard and the metal rungs of a disused playpark glinted a sickly pink in the fading light. Further back, near the edge of town, a smashed structure of brick and wood that looked like some kind of doctor's surgery or small hospital.

There were things moving in the mist. He couldn't make out shapes but blobs of white and pink shifted in the fog like lumps of solidified cloud, their grunts and whispers rising up to him on the breeze.

Beyond the village, separated from the ruins of the hospital by a vast, fog-enveloped graveyard, was the tall mutilated wreckage of an ancient church. The tower was enormous and turreted, the roof one of the only ones around without a great ragged scar in it. The great gothic building had been expanded, converted: gargantuan metal stacks rose bluntly behind it, supported by a compound of scaffolding and thick steel stilts. Bright red lights blinked behind dark windows, smoke rising steadily from a tall funnel of concrete to the left of the tower. Thick brass pipes rutted through the graveyard, bucking between headstones toward the church, where they looped around and into the scratched walls of the factory building attached to it. The whole structure was a brutalist-medieval nightmare of brick and iron, a refinery-cum-shrine with glinting spangles of stained glass and enormous black rivets punched into its sides.

That was where he had to go, he decided.

That was where he'd get his answers.

10

Brian came down the stairs quickly, almost plunging his foot into the black hole of the sixth step down and stubbing his bare toe painfully on the ridged, rutting slats of another. Nearly tumbling, he landed on the ground floor and stepped back into the abandoned, dark set-piece of the saloon. The light outside had truly begun to fade and the only thing coming in through the open, swaying wing doors was a wispy blanket of fog that seeped over the floorboards and billowed softly up the walls.

"All right," Brian said quietly, "you're above ground. That's half the battle."

Quickly he stepped past the bar counter and steeled himself to cross the room.

"Now you just have to—"

The boards groaned behind him.

Brian froze, his blood turning ice-cold as he stood in the middle of the abandoned saloon, every hair on his body raising an inch from his gooseflesh. He felt a stirring of fear in his stomach. For a second there was nothing, and then – slowly, unbearably – another of the floorboards complained under the weight of something significantly bigger than a rat.

Glacially, fancying he could hear a tiny crunch of bone against bone as he turned his head, Brian looked in the direction of the bar.

The crow had flown away, leaving a half-chewed mess of carcass on one of the barstools. The rest, upturned on the floor, rolled gently back and forth as fog trickled along their legs. The bar was just the same as it had been before; he was imagining things now, his brain addled by the cold and the terror that flooded his veins. He was going – or had gone – insane.

He was just turning to look away when the boards behind the bar counter squealed again.

"Oh, shit."

Brian watched in horror as a smooth, pale-white hand thrust up from the shadows behind the bar and slapped wetly down on the counter's surface. A small plume of dust erupted around the scrabbling, searching fingers as they raked across the wood.

Go, screamed the voice in Brian's head, *don't watch it, don't stand here, just* go.

But he couldn't move.

Frozen stiff, he looked on as the hand found purchase in the wood and the stubby, smooth fingers flexed, knuckles popping loudly. With great effort the creature hauled itself to its feet, slamming another hand onto the bar and straightening out like some deformed, pale bartender.

"Oh, *shit*."

The creature rolled its head on a flabby, white neck, one shoulder dipped below the other, its arms slender and bony. Its flesh was like cracked ivory, like the milky flesh of something drowned and left to bloat in the water. Its body was vastly misshapen, but he could tell it was meant to be human. Its chest was caved in and thin ribs poked sharply at the skin; its diaphragm and belly were round and fat and throbbed excitedly.

Slowly, it came around the bar, its bare feet slapping the floor wetly as it shuffled. It was naked; between bony hips, the small nub of a distinctly male sex organ was shrunken and smooth. The thing was hairless, covered in some thin coat of mucus that slithered over its joints and dripped onto the floor.

It had no face.

Its head was bald, and if there were ears they were somewhere beneath the skin; it had no eyes, no mouth, just faint, shallow indents and hollows like the lazy artificial "features" of a shop mannequin.

As it stepped into the soft late-dusklight filtering in through the door, its skin became a cloudy translucent haze. Brian could see chunks of tissue throbbing awfully in its torso, the wrinkled mess of its chest obscured by a network of flashing yellow nerves. Its faceless head flashed with the grinning imprint of a misshapen skull.

A collection of oddly-fused organs bundled into a body that didn't fit, the thing shambled forward zombielike and moaned, the hungry, almost sensual sound muffled through its skin. It reached out with both arms and Brian saw that it didn't have fingerprints, but smooth pads of flesh. No nails, no hair. it was a giant malformed milk dud with bones and body parts swimming about inside.

"What the fuck is happening?" Brian said, backing away.

As if sensing the nineteen-year-old's fear, the creature moved quicker, shuffling loudly forward and swiping blindly at the air. It stalked him across the saloon, stumbling over bumps and ridges in the floorboards.

"Get away from me," Brian whispered, fumbling behind him for a weapon, for anything. "Get the fuck away from me, you freak."

There was a thumping sound from the ceiling above him and he remembered the brief flash of white he'd seen in the bathtub. God, was there another one of these things up there?

His shin bumped an overturned table behind him and he glanced back, scrambled around a mess of furniture and looked desperately around for something to protect himself with. Seeing nothing, he bent down quickly and grabbed the nearest chair by the legs, knotting his fingers around stubby prongs of wood and heaving the thing into the air—

The creature moaned and lurched forward, swinging its shapeless smooth hand at Brian's head. He yelled and brought the chair arcing around, smashing it into the thing's semi-visible ribcage. There was a dull thump and the white-skinned beast staggered back, flopping onto another table. Brian cringed as a splinter surged deep into the pad of his thumb, a needle-like bolt of lightning shooting up into his arm. As the creature tried to stand he swung again, ploughing the chair's wooden back into its head.

There was no blood, but a definite *crunch* as something inside the creature's skull broke into pieces. It moaned again, the sound loud and awful despite being trapped inside the fleshy mask of its face.

"Yeah, take that, you milky bitch!" Brian yelled, turning the chair round in his hands and thrusting forward. The legs jabbed hard into the creature's ribs and stomach and it doubled over. "Fuck you! Fuck you, freak!"

He cried out as the creature grabbed the chair and, with an incredible and unexpected strength, wrenched it from his hands. Brian's breath hitched in his throat as the thing hurled the chair across the room, where it skidded across a dusty table surface and clattered into the wall. With a leering moan it shuffled toward him, punching a pale arm forward and grabbing Brian's throat.

Brian gasped as the creature squeezed, pushing upward until he was dangling three inches off the ground. "Fuck off!" he yelled, bringing a balled fist crashing down on the top of the thing's head. The creature's grip loosened and he struggled free of its grasp, staggering backward. He clutched at his neck, clamping a hand over the tender flesh, which already felt bruised and sore.

Brian reached for another chair, but the creature knocked his hand away before he could grab it. Backed into a corner, he ducked another swing and, panting, tried to wriggle away from the advancing white-skinned thing. His bare toe crashed into a table leg and he yelled, toppling forward and landing on his face in the dust. Fog rolled over him as he wheeled onto his back, looking up into the featureless moon-white face of the creature as it lurched toward him with both hands outstretched—

There was a titanic *crack!* and the thing's head exploded in a pulp of red and grey as something shining and black punched through it and smacked a cloud of splinters from the saloon wall.

Brian screamed, scrambling back as the white-skinned creature swayed forward, the ruined mess of its face spewing gore and chunks of half-knitted brain matter. It flopped into his lap and he shoved it away, cringing at the cold-jelly feeling of its flesh.

"*Ohh...*"

He looked desperately toward the wing doors. His frantic gaze settled on a tall, broad-shouldered figure on the porch. Time slowed down as the figure took a step forward, casting a long, shapeless silhouette onto the far wall.

The figure was drenched in shadow, a wide-brimmed hat cutting a vicious scythe of tattered leather across its brow. The figure's eyes flashed and Brian's gaze dropped, settling on something in its hand, an angular bone-shaped chunk of moonlit steel. The metal thing smouldered, a thin wisp of sooty smoke rising from the tip of a white-hot barrel.

Gun.

Brian grunted as the creature convulsed, falling back onto him, limp. Blood and slick, pink ichor poured out of the hole in its head.

"Help... me..." Brian gasped, pleading with the shape in the door as it stood watching the horrific scene. It was enormous, its face bathed in the shadow of that wide leather hat, its eyes flashing white and angry. The gun smoked in its hand, pale tendrils rising into and mixing with the moonlit fog. "Please..."

The shape ignored him.

Brian heaved the creature off, shoving with all his might and turning onto his front to crawl away from the bloody, milky pulp gushing onto the floor. He froze as he heard a dreadful, booming *click*, the sound of the stranger thumbing the hammer of a long, Colt revolver in its hand.

The shadowy shape swung its arm up and pointed the smouldering hunk of steel right between Brian's eyes.

58

11
The Lesson (I)

The floor was hard and uncomfortable, the carpet thin and threadbare beneath his rump, the lockers cold on his back. He sat with his knees pulled up to his face, his rucksack buried beneath his legs. He was sobbing.

Shapes moved in the very distant edges of Brian's periphery, older kids drifting from one classroom to another, just smudges of red and grey in the dull bleary fields of the corridor. The lunch bell was still ringing in his ears. Had that been minutes ago, or hours? How long had he been sitting here? Felt like hours. Legs numb. Head thumping.

The bruise across his ribs had spread and purpled already; he had seen it in the mirror in the boys' bathroom, pulling up his school shirt to see. He'd sat there in the headmistress' office pretending it didn't hurt. He'd wanted to cry. His jaw throbbed and his left eye was cupped in a hot, red blotch of puffy flesh.

Worse than all that, he'd pissed himself.

He smelled bitters before he heard his father's footsteps. Carl Cooper was a heavy man, six-foot-four with broad shoulders and a chest like one of the barrels of whiskey to which he was constantly puckered. His legs were like trunks. The corridor rumbled.

Before Brian could shrink further into himself a shadow loomed over him, blotting out the light from a row of narrow windows above the opposite lockers. There was a deep, gravelly sigh, and then the shadow crouched.

Brian looked up, face turned to one side in an attempt to hide his puffy black eye.

"Didn't fancy hitting him back this time?" his father grunted. His chin was pointed, his sallow cheeks thick with the dark grey muzz of an unruly beard. His hair was long and greasy, tied back behind square, leathery ears in a messy ponytail.

Brian swallowed. Teeth gritted tightly, he said, "He's bigger'n me."

"D'you think that stops your dad?" Carl Cooper said, crouched like a tiger on his thick, trunk-like heels. Steel toe-plates poked out of the ragged holes in his ancient, oily workboots like knives. A chaos of black-and-red ink sleeved his upper left arm, stormy clouds broken by lashing tentacles, the rapture of the Kraken spreading to his shoulder and jagged bolts of black ichor staining his neck. "D'you think your dad's scared of people bigger'n him?"

Brian shook his head. "I ain't you," he whispered.

I don't want to be.

"You're weak, boy. You understand that? This is gonna keep happening to you unless you start doing something about it."

"Yeah," Brian said.

"D'you hear me, boy? You gotta get your head outta those history books. They ain't gonna help you, understand? Kids're always gonna pick on the boy who prefers books to girls. You like your learning, you do it here. When you're at home, when you're on the playground… you talk about cars and toys and shit. Or you're gonna get beat."

"Why?"

"Don't matter why, that's the way it is."

"Okay."

"Come with me."

"Okay." *No.*

Brian's dad stood and he followed, reluctantly scooping his rucksack off the floor and gripping the straps, white-knuckled. "They

60

tell me this other boy was sent home early for kicking your guts in, is that right?"

"Yeah," Brian said, hobbling after his father down the corridor.

"You know where he lives?"

"No," Brian lied.

His father looked back, grinning wickedly. "Don't matter," he said. "*I* do."

12

The shape in the doorway lumbered forward, a great leather coat billowing around its bulk as it took a single, shuddering step into the saloon. The revolver in its hand was a black, pointing finger, steadily focused on the bridge of Brian's nose.

"Please," Brian whispered, his voice shaking. He knew there was a string of drool running down his chin but he couldn't swallow, couldn't breathe. "Please, I didn't do anything—"

The figure seemed to pause, as if seeing him for the first time. Its eyes were completely bathed in shadow now and its gargantuan shoulders blotted out the moonlight save for thin slivers that haloed its head, shapeless among a mane of thick, tangled hair and a ragged explosion of beard. The gun didn't tremble, but there was a hesitant nature in the way the thing spoke. "I never known one of you fuckers to talk before," it growled, its voice a gravelly rumble. Then it smiled, face cracking open, teeth flashing beneath the brim of its wide hat. "Never mind. You're all the—"

Brian yowled as something thumped down the stairs, a glistening white shape appearing behind the bar and lurching up, long fingers splayed into pointed nail-less spines. It was faceless, like the first had been, but the noise that erupted from somewhere within its skull was shrill and piercing enough to echo throughout the whole building.

"Fuck!" the shape with the gun yelled, swinging its arm round to point the revolver into the thing's featureless face.

The bathroom, Brian realised, scrambling to his feet and skittering across the saloon as another thundercrack boomed in his ears and the smell of gunsmoke played thrall with his senses. The thing that had been lying in the bathtub had slopped downstairs and was here, now, looming over the bar counter—

"You stay right where you are, shitheel!" the figure yelled as Brian ducked behind it. There was a *click* and the Colt fired again, a thick steel round smashing into the white-skinned creature's skull and spraying the shelves behind the bar with thick gobs of membrane. Brian ignored the shape and stumbled out of the door, tumbling over his ankles and rolling off the porch. A cloud of cool dust bloomed around him as the thick biting wind embraced his exposed skin, the smeared stripes of blood on his legs and arms tingling as they were caressed by needles of cold.

Brian gathered himself, straightening up and staggering drunkenly away from the porch. The sand scratched the soles of his feet as he moved, gunshots echoing in his skull. He turned the corner of the building and slammed his back into the wall as thundering footsteps crashed down the steps into the dust behind him.

"*Show yourself, cunt!*" the shape with the gun yelled. Its voice was male – human – and familiar somehow, though it had been ruined by years of shouting and heavy drinking. Was this one of the men that had found him in the library? One of the bastards who'd brought him here?

Brian gripped the wooden slats with the pads of his fingers and leaned back, risking a look around the corner of the saloon. Fog rolled around his ankles, seeping cold into his flesh.

He watched as the shape stepped forward, its long leather coat unfolding about thick, black-clad legs. The figure was like some kind of old west gunslinger, a giant with lanky hair billowing beneath the crest of his hat, bulges in his coat betraying the locations of more weapons strapped to his body.

This is a fucking nightmare, Brian thought.

The gunslinger stalked into the square, peering into the thick trails of fog between buildings as he approached the abandoned gallows. He paused for a moment before lowering the Colt.

Brian sunk back around the corner, squeezing his eyes shut and listening as the gunslinger's crunching footprints began to fade into nothing. Eventually he found the courage to open them again and turned his head away from the saloon and the square, looking down the street before him. Low ramshackle houses were stacked together in narrow rows, then a quarter-mile down the wide, sandy road, they became storefronts with overhanging awnings and porch rooves.

In the distance, the silhouette of the converted church loomed out of the fog, green lights blinking up its bulk and seeping into the night.

Drawing in a deep breath, he moved quickly away from the gunslinger and deeper into Peril.

13

Thick tendrils of fog coiled and bloomed around his calves as he hobbled cautiously down the high street. It was like wading through a river of ethereal, clammy swampwater, except the only things swimming in it were the little blossoms of dust and sand that kicked up when his bare, sore feet padded softly over the earth. The fleshy pads of his soles had been worn away to expose patches of red-raw muscle beneath; he wondered briefly if he'd have been desensitised to the pain by the time he'd shaved those muscles down to the bone beneath.

The storefronts were tall arched windows set beneath wooden porch covers; the first couple seemed empty, and the glass largely boarded up like the windows of the smaller houses around the square behind him. Where the boards on a narrow section of window had rotted – or been ripped – away, he stepped quietly onto the porch and peered inside, but saw only thick banks of darkness spilling over empty shelves. Glancing up at the sign above the door of the nearest building, he tried to read the faded lettering but was unsuccessful; from the pale green-and-blue paint peeling off the wood, though, he assumed it had once been a pharmacy.

A short way down Peril High Street was a small store with an entire window that hadn't been boarded up, and as he paused to look inside he was surprised to see that the building wasn't entirely empty. Indeed the remnants of an ancient window display gazed blankly back out at him: the shop had sold clothes, and a tall white mannequin stood on a grey plastic plinth, hands on her hips, a ratty red scarf around her neck. She was otherwise naked and there were smears of crimson marring her plastic breast and a swathe of dusty white hip. Her face was eyeless, the chin pointed and firm, the lips shallow and without detail. Brian hesitated by the window, considered stepping up onto the porch and finding a way in. The night air was chilling and even a scarf, as bare and thready as it was, would provide some comfort. But as he looked closer, he imagined shapes moving about in the darkness beyond the window display; things slithering between the shelves, lumpen abominations wriggling and squirming on the ceiling.

Probably just in his mind.

Still, he moved on, making it halfway down the street before another storefront caught his eye. Crossing the wide dirt road he looked left and right to make sure he wasn't being watched. No sign of the gunslinger, nor anything else. Not yet.

The store was like many of the others. Ramshackle, with dust gathering in great boughs on a slanted wooden roof and ragged holes in its awning; a mess on short stilts rutting out of the dust, the porch broken and crumbling to the ground, the wooden slats separated by great savage chunks of darkness.

The boards guarding the windows had been torn down and the glass shattered. Slivers and tiny shards of it sprayed the porch, many of them glittering in the shadows beneath. Inside, the shelves were bare save for a spinning rack upon which a single, tatty paperback book gathered dust. The sign above the door had completely worn away, the designs sanded down by the swirling dust of many years, and it was impossible to guess what the store might have sold.

A light flickered in a back room, a dim slice of amber that buzzed and crackled audibly. The other side of the shop, a till counter had long been abandoned. Dust-strewn cobwebs hung in a thick blanket across its surface and thick gobs of dark, red gunk had piled up around it to form sloping mounds of bubbling, mucus-covered flesh. Like moss at the trunk of a tree, they climbed until half the counter was covered in blood-red malformed growths, blooming colourfully like fungus.

There was a telephone on the counter. An old rotary-style thing painted peeling red.

He didn't know his mum's phone number off by heart, but he knew Josh's. they'd spent an afternoon testing each other, each taking a shot when they got a digit wrong until finally, in a slur of mispronounced noughts and sevens, Brian had finally gotten the whole thing.

The phone was his way out of here. He glanced again to the back door, slightly ajar, to the sliver of winking orange light peeking around the frame. The building had power. Therefore the phone had power. All he had to do was make it across the river of lumpen shadows across the shop floor and dial before anything leapt out at him from the dark.

Easy.

14

Brian eased a leg over the sharpened teeth of the windowframe and gingerly entered the store, grabbing the frame to steady himself and cringing as tiny slivers of glass pressed into his flesh. He was really going to have to get a tetanus shot when he got out of here.

Standing uneasily on the sill, he looked down to the floor. Moonlit glass behind him flared spikes of white about the edges of his vision, but the floor itself was coated with a thick murk of darkness. The darkness beneath his feet didn't look entirely flat, objects presumably having fallen from the shelves and gathered in neglected heaps on the floorboards. He remembered the black-and-white Nick Cave music video where a turgid ocean had been created from what looked like hundreds of bin liners, manipulated into flapping waves.

Gently, he held onto the ragged windowsill and lowered his foot to the floor.

His sole pressed into something spongy and warm and he recoiled, yanking his leg immediately back up. He wobbled, clamping a hand over his mouth to stifle the scream that had started to launch itself up his throat. The feeling of the thing on the floor clung to him, a phantom touch from something soft and gently-throbbing that, even in that dreadful tiny half-second, he knew had been lying there waiting for him for some time.

After a minute of quivering on the sill, a trembling window display that would only be successful in selling thick socks and year-long retreats at the local mental health centre, his eyes began to adjust to the dark inside the store.

"Oh, Jesus Christ," Brian whispered.

The floor between the window and the till counter – between him and the telephone – was carpeted with thick, bulging red shapes. A soupy, red topographical map of his despair was laid out from wall to wall, mounds and heaps of organic matter pressed tightly against a sheet of skin and badly-fused muscle that rippled and bubbled as he watched. He saw the pointed tips of ribs poking up through stretched orbs of kidney and flaps of cartilage. The membrane coating it all shivered gently in the wind, layers of dust shifting as the floor breathed and pulsed.

For a moment he wondered why he hadn't smelled anything, but then he realised that the thick stench of ripe meat was entirely clogging his throat and nostrils: it had been present since the underground chamber he'd woken up in; he'd just gotten used to it.

This carpet of organs and tissue laid out before him was just his life now.

Brian took a deep breath and stepped down again, this time more firmly. His foot sank into a waterbed-like mass of tissue, warm and slick on the very surface and scalding hot beneath. It throbbed around him, sucking him in to the heel, the skin stretching, but not breaking, the whole glutinous monstrosity elastic and welcoming.

Gagging, he lowered his second foot and stepped down from his perch on the sill, standing unsteadily in the spongy goop. His eyes lifted to the back door of the store and he paused: had the wind blown it open a little more, or had the shaft of light coming from back there always been so many inches wide?

Ripping his eyes away from the door, he attempted a step forward. The moist carpet sprung violently beneath him as he wrenched his first foot free of the clinging, hot glove of meat that had enveloped it. Groaning, he stepped toward the nearest shelf, reaching out for it to balance himself. Hauling his second foot forward, he ignored the wet shucking sound and tried not to vomit. The chasm of squirming, bulbous red between him and the till counter was streaked through with bolts of bone and veins of blue and purple, an intricate network of arteries threaded through knobs of skin and protruding half-knitted clumps of bicep and brain.

The floor was a sea of somebody's ruptured insides. In fact it felt that the building had prolapsed beneath him and a colossal abomination had been turned inside-out and smeared over every wooden surface. He couldn't help it: he threw up on the nearest shelf. A faded sticker told him in the half-light that newspapers had once been stacked there. Cheap, too: this place hadn't seen any commerce for a good few years.

Brian took another step, the shelf wobbling as he moved. It, too, had been half-consumed by tendrils and suckers, vines of globby red rising from the mass of spittle-flecked meatstuff to latch onto rotten wood and plastic. He could feel things moving about in the mass beneath him, subdued and lazy but alive nonetheless, and knew that he had to keep moving. It was like walking through a carcass, an enormous square corpse that had been flayed and separated and reconstituted just for him. It squelched beneath him as he moved, keeping his eyes on the telephone. There were no roaches or insects, and the cobwebs on the counter had long been abandoned, disintegrating so that the clumps of dust that had stuck to them were largely all that remained, an outer shell of fluffy mould protecting a hollow cavern with nothing inside.

The floor sucked at his feet as he limped across the store, the building growing darker around him the further he moved from the shattered window. The little slivers of moonlight that made it this far into the room bounced off wet lumps of bulbous red material beneath the translucent membrane that clapped onto the walls and trembled in the breeze. Taut corners of connective tissue snapped as he put pressure on denser patches of muscle, stepping between collections of bone that had been amassed from what must have been dozens and dozens of bodies.

Sickened, he clamped his hands on the till counter and heaved, doubling over it and dry-retching into the dark beyond.

Slumped on the counter, he scrabbled for the phone and jabbed his finger into the dial. With all the strength he could muster, he spun it all the way round. A dreadful snicking sound echoed into the store, too loud.

He heard a creak of wood and froze.

After nothing moved for a moment, he steeled himself and straightened his body. This was it. He was out of here. A quick call, and he was done. He was free.

What the hell would he say? He didn't know where he was. How far from them. How long he'd been here. How could they come get him, if he couldn't tell them the name of this place?

Refusing to acknowledge the sudden pit of unease that had opened up in his stomach, he swallowed and dialled the next digit. It didn't matter what he said. He had to let them know that he was alive. Finding out where he was would be easy: he just had to get *out* of here. Walk along the road until he came to the next town. Find another phone, call them again.

He just wanted to hear Josh's voice.

He could call the police, he thought, as he dialled the third number. The floor pulsed and throbbed around his enveloped feet. Somewhere behind him, an ancient hinge squealed. Three digits, and they'd have a much better chance of being able to track the call than anybody he knew.

No, Josh first. He dialled the fourth digit. The fifth.

The breeze shivered across his back and he turned his head to the window, looking out across the yawing red hole of the floor. The door at the back of the shop was half-open, a wide strip of blinking light stretching out onto the sloppy canvas of fused entrails and lighting a flailing tube here, an upturned eyeball glued to the carpet there.

He finished dialling and lifted the phone from its cradle, raising it to his ear.

It was ringing. Jesus Christ, it was ringing.

"Oh, holy balls," he whispered, closing his eyes and sobbing. It was all going to be okay. He was *done*.

"Hello?" came Josh's voice, weak and crackling through the speaker.

Holy fucking shit, Brian thought, *it actually worked. It's him.* He opened his mouth to reply, gallons of relief spilling hotly through his body.

"Hi—"

The store building shuddered as the back door swung open and slammed into the wall, the living carpet around him surging and grumbling as one. The telephone tumbled out of his hand and smacked the counter and he bent down to fumble for it, crying out as a gunshot exploded behind him and something whistled violently through the air where his head had been a moment before. Grabbing the phone, still attached to the receiver by a long, coiled cord, he whirled around to look.

Wide-eyed, he locked his gaze on the open door and watched in terror as the gunslinger stepped into a wide, flickering wedge of amber light, the revolver smoking in his hand.

"Got you, dickhead," the man whispered, spittle spraying the thick dark thatch of his beard.

"Fuck," Brian whispered, and without a second thought he threw the handset as far as he could, aiming for the gunslinger's moonlit silver-disc eyes and launching it from his hand with a yell—

There was a loud *snap!* as the cord went taut and tugged it right back toward him. Brian yelped as the handset clocked his shoulder and smashed into the receiver, the whole thing tumbling off the till counter with a crash.

"Fucking idiot," the gunslinger grunted, thumbing back the hammer and drawing.

A blood-smeared tendon punched up from the organic floor and snapped around the man's calf, constricting quickly as more lashed his boots and trousers. Like tentacles a series of the things shot up from the gyrating mass of squelching tissue and latched onto him, suckering to leathery material. The gunslinger growled and jammed his gun down, plunging the barrel into a throbbing lump of red and firing. The gunshot was muffled but Brian felt it in vibrations that coursed through the tissue clamped to his legs; it was this vibration that spurred him into movement, and he lurched back toward the shelves.

The gunslinger stomped forward, a pulsing section of floor popping beneath his heavy boot. Brian ducked behind the nearest shelf and slogged forward through the meaty, chewing swamp of the floor, lunging for the window. For the first time since he had been here – what, a couple days? A week? – he had heard Josh's voice. He had found a connection to home. Somebody that knew him.

And now this crazy bastard had taken Josh from him for a second time.

Fucker.

A shadow swelled over Brian's body and he looked up, eyes snapping wide open as he saw the gunslinger leering down at him from behind the shelves. "I got you now, shitknuckle," said the bearded man, long greasy hair in his eyes, the brim of his Stetson batted by clouds of dust that danced madly in the wind.

"Yagh!" Brian yelped, ploughing his body into the shelves. There was a great wet ripping sound as the connective tissue nailing the structure to the floor was severed in a few places, sheets of skin snapping and whipping his knees. The shelves tumbled into the gunslinger, knocking the huge man back into the spinning rack with the single paperback. The mountain with the revolver fumbled, swung his arm around—

Brian was halfway to the window. He leapt, pulling his feet hard with every step, the floor pulling back. The bullet soared past his ear, grazing flesh and producing a white-hot blast of pain that felt like a bee sting. The rest of the projectile smacked the wall.

The hammer clicked again. Brian yelled, launching himself at the sill, grabbing at it with both hands, lurching up.

He crashed through the shattered window and fell as the enormous crack of another gunshot rung in his ears.

The porch smacked his shoulder and Brian rolled onto his back, crumpling off the rotted wooden platform and falling on his stomach in the dust of the street. Desperately he looked up toward the window and watched in horror as the gunslinger loomed up in the frame, aiming again. Brian cringed – then his heart swung up into his mouth as the gelatinous mass of red and purple behind the gunslinger surged again, thick tendrils slapping the titanic man's back and whipping his arm away from the window.

Brian took his chance and unfolded from the floor – and fell down again, a nightmare of pain shooting up his leg. Terrified, he looked down to see that his bare leg was coated in a slick sheet of red, bubbling and spilling into the sand beneath him. It was warm.

Reaching down with a shaking hand, he wiped away some of the gloss, smearing it around the pale skin of his leg and gritting his teeth at the pain. Immediately more splurged from a dark, black eye of pain in the meat of his calf.

The bullet had sheared the edge of his leg as he'd gone through the window, punching a semicircle of bloody tissue out of his shin and fraying the skin around it.

He hadn't even felt it.

He felt it now.

Brian screamed as he grabbed the porch rail and heaved himself to his feet, ignoring the agonised yells of the gunslinger from inside the store and the thick, wet slurping sounds that accompanied them. The living carpet was consuming him.

Gripping the rail tight, Brian limped forward, no strength at all in his injured right leg. He dragged half his body along with the other half, using both hands to work his way along the wood. When he reached the end of the building he ploughed forward, hoping to make it to the next storefront with only one stride.

He crumpled, falling flat on his face as his leg screamed heat.

"*Fuck!*" he yelled, clamping a hand down on the wood. There was a sensation like something he imagined a burger patty might feel as it was smashed into a hot plate. He had to find something to use as a tourniquet – better yet, another phone to call a fucking ambulance and get himself out of here. When he looked down, he saw clumps of wet pink tissue squirming between his fingers, tiny tubes of broken muscle wiggling around the edges of the gunshot wound. A horrible suckered mouth-shaped hole in his calf, its lips dark with blood.

He screamed again as he stood, lunging into a half-limping, half-dragging assault on every fibre of his being. He staggered, blood spilling out of the sheared meat of his punctured limb into the dust. "*Eeyaaaaoooooaarghhh!*" he howled as his whole right side exploded with agony.

A window exploded off to his right.

Almost crumpling again, Brian's head whipped around and he shrieked as a wall of shattered glass blew into the street, some of the smaller shards sprinkling his chest and legs. From the darkness behind the window a gaggle of shapes emerged, slopping onto the porch of a store that (based on the gold and green of the faded, peeling sign) might have been a Harrods-inspired gift shop at one point. The first shape was a white-skinned creature without a face, a human-shaped vacuity with reaching, smooth fingers and thick blue veins pulsing across its chest and neck. Behind it, three more of the things clambered over the broken glass in the frame – but these were only half-formed, their arms and patches of their skin knitted into that semi-transparent pale fabric but the rest uncovered, exposed lumps of bone and muscle melted together so that they looked like they had been ripped apart and reformed several times. More of them tumbled out of the window as Brian watched, some of them wearing the same white skin of the featureless creature leading the pack, others nothing but shambling mounds of bone and meat.

"Ohh, shit," he breathed, howling again as he dragged himself forward another step.

Another window burst open, this time to his left and further down the high street. More of the things tumbled out, grinning skulls propped on spinal columns with striated red torsos and grabbing bony hands; deformed one-armed or one-legged shapes of swirled white and red, mucus dribbling from puncture wounds in their flesh-like forms.

Brian lurched into an awful shuffling half-run and screamed – for all four of the feet he made it before he collapsed onto his stomach and the horde descended on him.

15
The Lesson (II)

If the walk across the school car park seemed to take hours, the drive to Zach Broome's house took an eternity.

An eleven-year-old Brian sat in the passenger seat, nervously chewing the inside of his cheek as he stared out of the window. A blur of beige and green streaked past the old Hyundai as his father cruised them through the outskirts of town and into a complex of council houses and apartments flanked by two birdshit-smeared billboards. Bright clumps of geraniums splashed the verges with red and pink, the newly-laid road winding through the complex smooth and pleasant to drive on.

They pulled up on the kerb outside a nondescript terraced house, and Brian turned his head forward to avoid looking out into the lawn. "I don't want to do this," he said as firmly as he could, his eyes locked on the dimpled grey plastic of the dashboard.

"I don't care," his father said quietly. Carl Cooper heaved up the handbrake and turned off the engine, and for a moment they sat in the silence and the heat. The old car smelled like metal and beer. "Come on. We didn't come out here for nothing, boy."

"I don't want to. I want to go home."

Then there were fingers in his hair and Brian yelped quietly as his head was roughly twisted around to face his father's. Claws pressed into the soft base of his skull and the pressure made him want to cry. "We don't go home until this is done," Carl growled. His breath stunk of meat and his eyes were tiny silver points. "D'you hear me?"

"You're hurting me—"

"Do you hear me?" Carl snapped, every word punctuated by thick gobs of spittle flying from his lips. He twisted his fingers hard into the boy's hair.

"Yes," Brian said desperately, "yes, I hear you."

"Good." Carl's fingers slipped away, leaving a tufted knot of hair standing up stiff at the back of Brian's head. The big broad man smiled: no teeth; just thin, black lips. "All right. Get out."

Brian unclipped his seatbelt and scrambled out of the car, almost falling onto the pavement. His ribs still hurt and the puffy red ring around his eye had turned an ugly blue. Before he could straighten up his father had bunched a fist into the back of his shirt and hauled him to his feet, marching him toward the lawn gate.

Brian looked up at the house and cringed, his heart sinking deep into his stomach and shrinking into a knotted ball of worry. There was a scream as the gate was opened for him; the house loomed over him like some buffeted tower, gargoyles leering down from the narrow chimney stack. Lightning seemed to flash across the small upper-floor windows and he realised he might be having what his mother had called a Panic Attack. He was moving forward but his legs weren't under his control, his breaths ragged and frequent like he was sobbing. "Stop," he tried to say, "Please, stop—"

The words didn't come.

"Ring the bell," his dad said gruffly.

Brian didn't remember jabbing the button but suddenly the sound was echoing in his ears, the booming chime of the doorbell tolling like a thousand tuning forks. He staggered back from the doorstep and time passed. He wasn't sure how much. Hours? *Breathe.* Chest pounding. Whole body tremoring with every heartbeat. *BREATHE.*

78

His body went still as the door swung open.

Petrified, he watched the tall, angular shape of Zach Broome's father lurch into the frame. His eyes drifted up the pinstripes of a crisp blue business suit and reached Mr Broome's face, which was pinched and pale. His eyes were beady sparks of grey beneath narrow eyebrows, his hair neatly combed. Slowly the man reached into his jacket pocket and withdrew a pair of round spectacles, settling them on the bridge of a beak-like nose.

"Ah," he said, looking first at Brian's father then at the boy on the doorstep. Tilting his body a little, he called back into the house: "Zachary! There's somebody here to see you!"

Brian could feel his father's eyes burrowing right through him as he waited, not saying a word. The air between him and the open door felt hot and thick. Mr Broome slid his hands into his pockets, returning his gaze to Brian's father.

"You know, of course," he drawled, "that my boy was provoked."

"By what?" Carl laughed bitterly. "This little wimp's never thrown a punch in his life."

"Not according to my boy." Behind Mr Broome, the thumping sound of footsteps crashing down the stairs. A shadow appeared in the hallway then, seeing who was standing outside, came tentatively to the door.

Zach stood beside his father, pudgy cheeks spattered with freckles. He looked through narrow eyes at Brian and reached up to tug his dad's sleeve. "What are they doing here?"

"What are we doing here, Brian?" Carl Cooper snarled.

Brian was frozen to the spot. His eyes were locked on Zach Broome's face, his belly turning in circles. Anger flared in deep bolts of red across his vision. He didn't want to do this.

"Brian," his father said.

Brian shook his head. He had the power here. He could smash the fucker's face in and Zachary Broome's father wouldn't do a thing about it, not with Brian's hulk of a dad standing three feet from him. They all knew that Brian had never done a thing to provoke anyone. He was justified. He was *right*.

He deserved this.

Slowly, he looked back into his father's face. Carl's eyes were set and the pupils swum in viscous pools of bloody milk. He nodded, head bobbing on a thick, muscular neck.

"Go on, son," Carl Cooper said, flashing sharp teeth and gums stained yellow from chewing nicotine.

Brian's heart pounded. "No," he whispered. "I. Don't. Want. To."

He did. Oh, more than anything, he wanted to.

But he wasn't his dad.

"The fuck did you say to me?" Carl hissed.

"Come on, Zachary, I'm not going to stand here and watch this," Broome said, laying a hand on the bully's shoulder and turning to step back inside.

"You fucking stay there," Carl said, his voice suddenly eighteen decibels louder and raised in pitch by half an octave. "Brian, is this the little shit that beat on you or not?"

Brian looked Zach dead in the eye and swallowed nervously. "Yes."

"Then give him back what he gave you."

A beat. Then, more confidently than he felt: "*No.*"

"Fine," Brian's father spat, shoving Brian to one side and marching forward.

Broome swung his body in front of Zach's, eyes widening. "I'll tell you what, mate, if you even *think* about laying a hand on my boy—"

Carl thrust a hand up and punched his palm into the man's chin, immediately clamping Broome's narrow jaw in a vice-like fist. "Wouldn't dream of it," he growled, and there was a sick, wet *crunch* as he swung his arm to the side and smashed Broome's head into the doorframe.

Brian yowled on the lawn, scrambling to his feet and lurching forward. "Stop it!" he yelled. The suddenly-tiny shape of Zachary Broome backed into the hallway, screaming.

Carl Cooper slammed his knee into Broome's groin with a dull *thump* and looked back at Brian, teeth gritted, eyes bulging with rage.

"You stay back, boy!" he hissed. "Daddy's got this one."

Brian lunged for his dad's leg and Carl swung an elbow back, clocking the boy in the chin and sending him sprawling backward, a hot pool of warmth seeping over his tongue. He landed on his back and looked up in horror as his dad turned his attention back to the man in the doorway, snarling like an animal.

"Nobody touches my boy but me," Carl Cooper whispered, and with a sound like a gunshot he squeezed, still gripping Broome's lower jaw in his vice-like claws. The crack of bone echoed and Broome wailed as broken teeth slipped down his throat.

Brian watched from the lawn, sobbing and heaving, as Broome crumpled, hands rushing to his broken jaw. He slurred something that might have been *Call the police!* except the only thing that really came out of his mouth was a rush of bubbling, bright red.

Carl turned away from the door and reached out a hand. It was white and speckled with blood. "Come on, boy," he said quietly. "Daddy's got another lesson for you when we get home."

16

Brian rolled onto his back and punched upward, smashing his knuckles into the faceless skull of the creature that had leapt onto his torso. Its head and neck were masked in white, veiny skin like the cowl of some sickening vigilante but the rest of it was all red-raw muscle and meat, tendons holding it together; bony knuckles popped out of sinuous hands as it splayed its fingers ready to claw him apart.

Yowling as the weight of another creature pinned his shot leg to the ground, Brian launched his elbow into the first's neck and sent it sprawling away. A third clambered onto his chest as he kicked at the second with his good leg, and then a set of teeth clamped to his shin and he yelled in pain as he lost count of the manic things attacking him.

"Fuck off!" he screamed, heaving his whole upper body upward and smashing his forehead into the skull of the next beast. It tipped backward, exposed skull cracking open as the malformed organs of its chest – a bundle of kidneys and livers glued to the purplish sac of one bloated lung – spilled up out of its ribcage. Another of the creatures bit down on his arm and he looked down to see something that looked like an entire skeleton riddled with cancerous heaps of muscle and skin, tearing savagely at his flesh. With his free hand he punched it square in the skull, briefly loosening its toothy grip on his meat, but another had already grabbed his neck with a white-skinned, nail-less hand and he couldn't breathe, couldn't see past the silhouette of another looming down on him, its face blank except for an eyeball in its mouth that it had bitten and that was slowly deflating and rolling up into its jaw.

He tried to stand but the weight on his body was too much and the agony in his leg was unbearable. A pile of organs in the shape of a man was lapping hungrily from the wound while two more fought over his good leg, slapping each other away and grazing his skin with half-formed teeth and bony fingers.

It was an onslaught of fucked-up biology classes in human form, combinations of organs that shouldn't have complimented each other bundled into loose skin until they at least made the vague shape of a person, each one roughly his own height and weight, many of them missing legs and a couple headless abnormalities shuffling blindly about.

A parade of half-arsed and discarded human rejects. Zombies of muscle and bone that scrambled and clawed over each other to get to him.

Brian howled as another slammed its head into his and something cracked loudly.

The air around him was suffocated with grunts and moans, hungry slopping sounds and anguished whines as the horde surrounded their prey, stamping him into the dirt, swiping each other away as they hungrily closed in on his body. With his last scrap of strength Brian slammed the heel of his hand into the jaw of a faceless white-skinned creature and followed through, punching its head into the stomach of another behind it – this one with a grappling arm in place of its left leg and a yawing, tube-filled stump where the arm should have been – so that both of them tumbled into a third and its suckling mouth was separated from the wound in his leg. It was no good: as the three abominations fell away a fourth and fifth leapt into the opening and clawed desperately at his gut, savaging the material of the bloody hospital gown he'd found below ground.

A *crack!* and Brian's face was spattered with hot, viscous blood. He sucked in a breath as a weight fell off his chest and batted his elbow into the smooth groin of a white-skinned zombie-thing kneeling on his neck. Another *crack!* and the grinning skull of another exploded. All at once the street was booming with gunshots, tendrils of blood ripping out of the necks and faces of the savages on his body as bullets pounded through them one by one. Gasping, Brian lurched up to see the gunslinger marching in his direction, the dark leviathan of a man swinging his Colt left and right. There was a brief respite in the thunder of gunshots and he cocked his arm back, ejecting the cartridge and filling it again with a handful of glinting streaks. Before Brian could react he was shooting again, punching his finger back into the trigger without touching the hammer, every shot ringing out.

Brian scrambled back as he was showered with blood and flecks of white-pink flesh, bullets flying above him.

When the silence came, he and the gunslinger was alone.

On his back, Brian raised his shaky hands and gazed up at the gunslinger. All around him horrible mutations lay in the dust, fog already consuming their bodies, blood pooling out of them and spilling into the earth.

There was a pause.

The revolver was pointed at Brian's right eyeball. His leg burned. This was it.

Slowly, he swallowed.

"Please," he whispered, his whole body run through with bite-marks and gouges, "tell my family what happened to me."

The gunslinger stared at him for what felt like a long time, his thumb resting on the hammer, the pad of his gloved finger pressed firmly to the trigger. His face was horribly scarred, Brian realised, the beard patchy where his cheeks were crisscrossed with white tissue. His eyes were dull and lifeless, his teeth gritted in a square, moveless jaw.

The titan lowered his arm. Nodded toward the end of the street. "The factory," he growled, indicating the green lights of the converted church. "That where you're headed?"

Brian nodded.

"You won't find anything in there you like," the gunslinger warned him.

"Answers," Brian choked. "I just want answers."

"Oh, plenty of answers in the factory, that's for sure."

"Then I have to—"

"Fine," the gunslinger said quietly. He raised a hand. "I won't argue."

"Can you help me get out of here?"

There was a long silence. Something twitched in the dirt, a little way from where Brian lay in a cloud of blood and sand.

"No," the gunslinger said finally. "Find your answers, shitknuckle. If you're sure you want them."

"And then you can help me get home?"

"And then you won't *want* to get home," the gunslinger said. Spinning the revolver around his finger, he clapped the cartridge loose and emptied five of the bullets into his hand. Pocketing them, he tossed the gun into the dirt at Brian's feet. "You'll need this."

"Who are you?"

"You'll figure it out," said the gunslinger, turning away. As he did the folds of his coat billowed and Brian caught a glimpse of more weapons strapped to his belt. He swallowed.

When the gunslinger had walked away a good twenty or thirty feet, Brian picked up the gun with a trembling hand, wincing as pain shot up his wounded leg.

Gingerly, he checked the cartridge. One bullet left.

You'll need this.

He turned his head, whole body straining, to look up at the church-cum-factory building at the edge of town. It was all in there. Answers. The truth.

As he lay there, he caught a glimpse of something shuffling behind the storefronts: a hunched creature with narrow legs and blood dripping from its mouth and hands. Moving quietly, stalking toward the factory.

There was something horribly familiar about the shape. He

85

shuddered it off.

You won't want *to get home.*

Brian had a sick feeling, deep in his gut, that the gunslinger might be right.

17
The Lesson (III)

Brian yelped as his father shoved him through the open door into the living room, tumbling onto his hands and knees on the carpet. A fire crackled across the room; his mother was already standing from her place on the sofa, both hands moving to her face. Beside her another woman – one Brian briefly recognised in a flash of respite from the thumping pain obscuring his vision as somebody from his mother's bridge circle – scrambled back in her chair, her face immediately turning white.

"Jesus, Carl, what the fuck?" Brian's mother yelled. She turned to the other woman and said, "Call for an ambulance, Jen. Now."

"I should go—"

"Now, Jenny!" Mrs Cooper screamed. Turning to Brian's father, her face flashed with thunder. "What the hell have you done?"

Brian looked up through the swollen nix of his black eye and watched the spiky silhouette of Carl Cooper stumble forward, both his fists clenched. "Boy needed teaching something," he mumbled. Or maybe he wasn't mumbling, and Brian's ears were bleeding. His ribs ached like hell, his head pounding where Carl had smashed it into the dashboard. There was blood and skin in his teeth.

Brian said, "Uuunnh…"

"Carl, this is serious. He needs to go to hospital right now." Mrs Cooper turned. "Jenny, the ambulance?"

"On their way," the other woman said, fumbling with her phone pressed to her ear. "Thirteen minutes."

"Tell them to fuck off," Carl slurred. He had drunk half a can of Stella on the way home; it would have been more if the rest hadn't sloshed over the wheel and spilled over his jeans. His back was covered in sweat; the fire buzzed angrily. For all Brian could see it seemed to have consumed the entire far wall of the living room.

His mother's hands were on his arms, then, and she was crouching down in his face, shaking him gently. "Brian? Brian, love? Can you hear m—"

Something smashed the left side of Mrs Cooper's face and she disappeared. Jenny screamed, rushing across the room, the phone hanging off its cord, swinging violently in a wide pendulum and lit by the fire – *you're feeling sleepy* – and then Brian's mother's face was replaced by another, darker face, and he sobbed as a thick set of fingers knotted around his neck and squeezed.

"You listen to me, boy," said Carl Cooper. His voice was like the voice of a snarling dog. His eyes were the firelight on the wall, greasy and hungry and orange. "You listen, 'cause this is important. You got to stand up to these bullies, you know. You got to fight. When they give you something nasty, you give it right back to 'em. You understand?"

Brian said nothing. Couldn't have, even if he wanted to.

"And you know why?" Carl slurred through a grinning maw. Brian could smell the danger on his breath. "'Cause there's a lot more of 'em than there are of you. You got to start fighting back, 'cause if just *one* of 'em lands a punch, then it don't take many more to put you in the dirt. You hear me?"

Brian gasped for air. A shadow lurched up behind Carl Cooper, something long and heavy in its hand.

"You got to start *fighting*, boy. 'Cause if you don't—"

The lamp shattered on the back of Carl's skull and his eyes bulged, his grip loosening momentarily. Brian sucked in air and kicked up into his dad's stomach, his foot thrusting hard into soft tissue. Carl swayed, then fell.

Jenny stood over them, looking from Brian's mother to his father and back to him. The lamp in her hand was broken and covered with blood.

"He'll be fine," she whispered dumbly, and the lamp fell from her hand.

The fire crackled.

18

Brian limped to the fence surrounding the churchyard and laid a hand on the wood, his body weight crumpling forward as his leg buckled again. Panting, he squeezed the gun in his hand and looked up.

He shivered as the wind grabbed his bare legs and slipped into the hospital gown. There was a poorly-stitched pocket in the hip of the gown and he slid the gun inside, hardly obscuring it but at least giving his weak knuckles a break.

The churchyard was bleak, a labyrinth of leaning headstones – all of them worn down so that, even if he could read through the pumping haze filling his vision, he wouldn't have been able to make out the names; dozens of them clumped together around a few large patches of scarred black earth – struggling up a hillock of mossy blue ground. The fog slipped lazily between narrow black obelisks and chunky slabs of cracked concrete. Scrappy trees thrust out of dry, broken dirt.

The looming church was a once-proud medieval building encased in the glittering metal shell of a vast production unit. It exploded into the sky, a rapture of scaffolding and curved riveted surfaces, smoke billowing from tall funnels into the ink-black clouds and blotting out the moon. Green-lit windows winked down at him.

A door in an enormous, silo-like outer building was wide open, smoky red light pouring out into the churchyard. An arched welcome sign bleeding out through the dark.

As he lurched toward the gate, he noticed that a great glossy streak of red had been painted on it: a bloody handprint.

Gently he laid his own hand inside the mark, swallowing as he clamped his fingers down on hot, wet wood.

Looking back up at the factory, Brian swung the gate open and limped forward.

PART III

THE

ABOMINATION

FACTORY

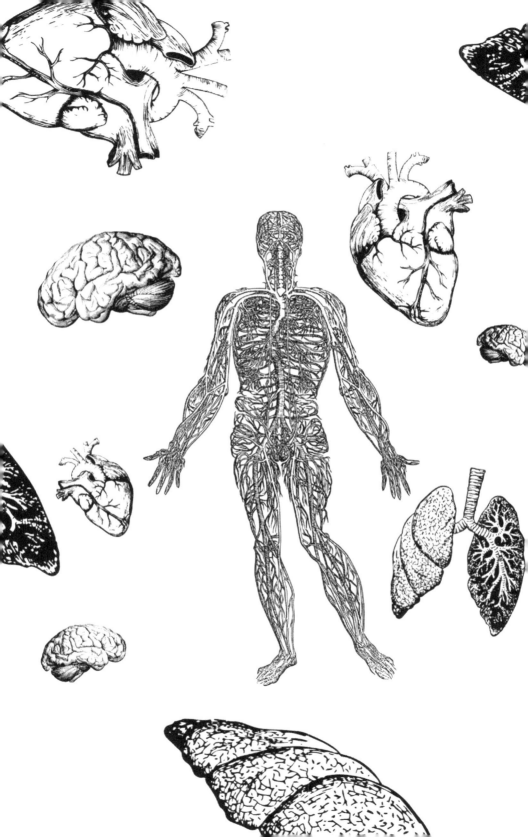

19

The door swung open with a grinding metallic scream and he stumbled forward, almost collapsing into a wedge of flickering green light inside the corridor. Lurching out of the dark, the young man reached up with a trembling hand to paw at a gluey mess of blood and spittle covering his chin. Speckles of red dotted the wall as he flung a gob of the tangy copper-scented concoction off his face.

Swallowing, the boy let the door close behind him and looked into the dark.

The corridor was long and curved to the right, the walls bulging outward as though he had found himself in a tall steel pipe. Behind him the door clicked softly into the frame and the ringing of the hinges finally stopped echoing in his ears. After a minute or so his hearing had attuned to the softly-booming walls and the faint rattling above and below him, a constant electronic whirr seeming to punch up into the floor and spread through the metal. The whole place trembled persistently as he stepped forward.

He was grateful for the smooth, cool steel of the floor: the soles of his feet had been shredded to bits and he left a sticky trail of blood behind him as he shuffled forward. It was not warm inside the corridor, but it was, at least, not as cold as it had been below ground. Green halogen bulbs winked and flickered on the walls, evenly spaced (though some of them had long-ago shattered or died in their greasy glass casings, leaving absences of black behind dusty metal grilles) and just powerful enough to each illuminate a few feet of tunnel with a burry, emerald halo. Thin copper pipes twisted and buckled above him, many of them scratched and rusted, some broken and gently seeping clots of grey gas into the air. As the boy moved forward and started around the bend in the corridor, he lifted a corner of the ripped, bloody hospital gown to his nose and mouth to cover them. Just in case. He exposed his legs and genitals as he did, but he barely spared them a thought. Anybody watching his progress through the dreadful compound in which he'd found himself had probably seen far worse by now. Besides, he was fairly confident he was at least half-dead. What did a little indecent exposure matter at this point?

Wary of the fumes above him – and finding that even the pale green glow of the blinking bulbs on either side was almost blinding after the darkness that had accompanied him so far – the boy moved slowly. His eyes skirted every square inch of steel and he noted that the corridor wall was a patchwork of grilled vents and riveted strips of iron. Every inch of the tunnel had been repaired and remade; this operation – whatever it was – had been running for a long time.

Decades, it looked like.

But was it *still* running? There was nobody in here. He hadn't caught so much as a glimpse of the enormous black-gloved figures who'd taken him from the university. Only the fleeting movements and whispered groans of other distant shapes shuffling about the compound. He was fairly certain they weren't in charge.

So who was?

The boy glanced behind him as a thick, dry *clunk* boomed through the tunnel. Frozen in place, he scoured the green-lit hallway for any sign of movement and found none; deciding that this was probably the kind of building that just made those sounds whenever it felt like it, he turned his head and continued. The tunnel kept swerving around to the right and he followed it tentatively, his heartbeat thumping loudly in his temples.

Something scuttled in the dark behind him.

Swallowing, the boy ignored the sound and continued. Small sounds like that were okay, he had decided. It was the heavier sounds that warranted concern. Pressing forward, he steeled himself as the corridor straightened out and squinted into the dim green light at the end of the tunnel.

A door hung slightly ajar, the arched ceiling above thick with clumps of dust that clung to ancient cobwebs. The frame was smacked through with a couple dozen bolts and spattered with rust; the hinges had worn to slivers of the original metal pins. It had probably been locked at one point, but the ever-present trembling of the building had shaken it loose.

Or something opened *it*, the rational part of his brain – continually shrinking, he supposed grimly – piped up.

"There's no one here," he whispered as he approached the door, tilting his head to peer through the gap. Nothing but darkness beyond, pale knobs of white smeared and swirled into the shadows. "There's no one here. Just you."

No one here.

The scuttling thing behind him crept forward, its tiny paws *tck-tck-tck*ing on the steel floor.

Just you.

The boy reached for the door, laying his hand on the knob and drawing a deep breath before pushing it slowly open. Inside, a wide, circular room with tall steel walls, intricate and twisted networks of thick black cables running up them to a central node in the ceiling. More wires, some red and frayed, a couple sparking where they had been severed, dangled from the node and down into a bank of desktop monitors upon a wide, horseshoe-shaped desk in the centre of the room. Glancing down, the boy saw that the thicker cables stapled to the walls also snaked under the desk and thrust up into the cavity beneath. About half of the monitors were dead, the screens black and vacuous, but the other half—

The boy yelped as something grabbed his calf.

"What the—" he yelled, looking down as a knot of claws dug into his flesh and twisted. "Ow!"

His eyes widened as the scuttling thing coiled tightly around his shin and squeezed. It was a hand. There was no arm attached; it had been severed just beneath the wrist, and the grisly stump bulged where nubs of bone pressed against the loosened skin. Tiny wriggling tendrils of flesh writhed at the edges of the stump, spattered with red and twisted into dark, wet tangles. The fingers were long and deformed, but distinctly human. The knuckles were all misplaced but they seemed to function, a couple of spares knocking about in the back of the hand and scraping each other as the awful bloody thing raced up his leg and dipped behind his knee, propelling itself by digging its nails into his skin and slithering after them.

The boy yelped as the hand ploughed up the inside of his thigh, finally batting at it with his own hand. He smacked it off easily and cringed at the dull, wet *smack* of flesh on steel as it was flung to the floor a few feet away. Staggering backward into the room with all the monitors, he went to shut the door.

Too slow.

The hand scrabbled forward and leapt up onto his knee, punching into the kneecap with such force that the boy's leg nearly buckled. Before he could react it had jumped from his hip to his chest and then it was crawling up his neck and clamping down, hard. He gasped for air as it crushed his windpipe, grabbing at the thing with both hands and stumbling blindly into the nearest wall. He tried to dig his fingers into the space between his throat and the clammy palm of the thing but it had almost suctioned itself to him. The severed wrist flopped wildly, spattering his own forearm with gobs of gloopy wet blood. The fingers curled into claws and punctured his neck in four places, beads of blood blooming around the sharp and chipped nubs of its nails.

The boy's eyes rolled up into his head as he pulled and yanked at the hand, trying desperately to separate it from his neck. It squeezed tighter, compelled by an insane strength, and in the very corner of his vision he saw flashes of white bone dancing in the wet tissue of its stump. He swallowed madly at the air but every time his throat shrunk, even slightly, the hand constricted its grip until it became entirely impossible to breathe. Clouds of blackness surged into his vision and he sunk down the wall, wrenching at the thing with all his strength. It was still gripping, still squeezing, and he tried something different—

A wave of repulsion crashed through him as he plunged his fingers into the sloppy wet mess of the stump, slipping them violently between knots of bone. The hand twitched, nerves involuntarily tightening and snapping open as his fingers worked the warm meat of the hand like a sock puppet. He tried to fling it away, sucking at air and blinking away the inky clouds in his eyes; the hand was firmly glued to his own and instead of throwing it he smacked it hard against the wall with a resounding *thwump*.

The thing was still twitching, the fingers grasping at his face, and with his free hand he gripped them tightly. Drawing in a hard breath, he twisted.

There was a dull *crack* as three of the four fingers dislocated. Surging with adrenaline, the boy let go of them and lunged down with his jaws, biting cleanly through two of them with one movement. His teeth sheared easily through weak bones and he was reminded vaguely of the sensation of biting through a carrot – then there was warmth in his mouth and something scraping his cheek and he realised that the two severed fingers curled up on his tongue were about to slide down his throat if he didn't spit them out. Disgusted, he bent down his head and threw them onto the floor in a gob of bloody spittle. Recoiling with disgust, he looked down at the hand in which his own fingers were buried and saw that the remaining fingers – and thumb – were still twitching. The tiny stumps where he had bitten off the other fingers were gently drizzling blood and a sickly yellow fluid. Exposed knuckles shone through slivers of torn muscle.

Repulsed, he did what he had to do.

20

The boy stood shakily over the monitors, gripping the edge of the horseshoe-shaped desk with both hands. His body was weak and shivered uncontrollably; even the task of lifting the overturned office chair at his feet seemed like too much effort.

As his eyes moved from one screen to the next, the limp splotch of pinkish flesh on the floor behind him twitched wetly. A collection of half-chewed nubs that had once been fingers were scattered around the savaged clump of palm that remained. Blood pooled around them.

The monitors were ancient and bulky, each screen bulging out in the middle and framed with clamps of matte grey plastic. Any identifying marks or model numbers had been sanded off the machines, but many of the screens had been dressed with a small circular sticker labelling it with a number from one to twenty-four. Screens one, three, five-through-nine and a bunch of the high teens were dead, which the boy supposed probably had something to do with the frayed wires above him. The desk itself and the tops of the monitors were covered with a thick blanket of dust.

On screen two (the sticker was peeling, but the permanent marker had blistered a lazy black *Z* onto the monitor beneath as though whoever had written it had done so *after* sticking it to the plastic) was a hazy image of the subterranean chamber where he had woken up. He could only make out vague shapes, but the door he'd come through was there on the left, and he could see the flash of a ladder poking down on the right.

The heaps of organic matter and bone piled up against the walls seemed to be moving, throbbing on the grainy black-and-white screen.

"Is this live?" he whispered to himself as his eyes flitted to the next working screen. Here the camera seemed to have been positioned behind the counter of an abandoned store; there were coils of rope hung on hooks on the far wooden wall, and the shelves were mostly empty; a sparse collection of what looked like power tools made for square, boxy shapes in the shadows.

Screens ten and sixteen seemed to show the same room from different angles: from what he could see, it was a large, round chamber with enormously high walls and hooded halogen lamps swinging slowly from the ceiling. The floor was made of plated steel and in the centre of the room a wide, round grille – about six or seven feet across, perhaps – covered a whirring bloom of shadows that he presumed was some kind of spinning fan.

The walls were covered in blood. Thick, dark gobs of it oozed down, black and dry and stained permanently.

Another screen showed what looked like a schoolyard, fenced off: through the chain-links he saw shambling white-skinned shapes clawing at each other. Dozens of them, some ripped open so that their guts spilled out, others missing limbs or heads. He shuddered.

Three screens at the bottom of the flickering bank seemed to deliver a feed of various darkened hallways and corridors in the building he was currently in.

Screen twenty-three was mostly dark, but the image was just about discernible if he leant in and squinted hard. Doing so, he made out a faintly-glowing doorway, wide open and swinging in the breeze, with what looked like a faint cluster of streetlights in the distance.

Escape.

He had been avoiding looking at the last screen, having already caught a glimpse of the pale shapes on the monitor. Now he looked, tipping down his head and locking his eyes on the flickering banks of static that rolled up and down the glass. There was a distinct, swimming wooziness to the image that made him wonder if he wasn't making half of all this up. But somehow, he knew it was real.

A dark, long room, with narrow strips of fluorescent light bleeding across the walls. The room was packed wall-to-wall with monitors, machinery – and tall, faintly-pulsing canisters of soft, white light. It was hard to make them out, but they looked like tanks. Big cylindrical fish-tanks, each one filled with a pale fluid that, even on the grainy monitor image, seemed to froth and bubble as he watched.

A shadow flitted past one of the screens. As he moved his head to look, he noticed that another – the camera pointed at an open door on the outer wall of the building – was also busy with movement. He watched in horror as a blood-covered shape slithered up to the door and pressed a sloppy hand on the metal. Coming inside.

Coming for him.

The boy's eyes flitted from screen to screen, returning again and again to the monitor which seemed to be showing him a way out. Right there in front of him, an open door and signs of life – civilised life – beyond…

But even if it was real, how could he find it? How would he know where to look?

As if in answer, there was a distinct *smack* behind him. He turned to look and saw that the dismembered hand had moved a few inches closer and turned onto its back, palm presented upward as if in some sacrificial offering to an invisible palm-reader. The boy swallowed, watching the fingers as they twitched softly in the pool of blood that had sprayed the floor.

His eyes drifted up and relief flooded his chest.

Sprayed across the back wall where he'd come in – he'd never have seen it if he hadn't turned around – was a map.

"Holy fucking shit," he breathed.

A white, chalky rectangle seemed to represent the church building he had glimpsed on one of the screens, and he imagined that the circular shape next to it was the factory building. A network of tube-like scrawls might have been the tunnels and corridors connecting the two. Panning out, the map was divided into areas that looked like streets and a small village square – Christ, was this place really as big as this? – and in the middle of that he saw a couple of larger shapes, either of which might have been the schoolyard and building from the monitor behind him.

Squinting, he saw numbers scrawled in red across the map. His eyes widened.

Stepping closer, he looked desperately for number twenty-three. *Escape.*

He found it, nestled in the northeast corner of the factory building. Not far from him. and in fact, now that he was focusing on that part of the map, he saw that there was a faint white smudge indicating the room in which the monitors were situated (somebody, in tiny strikes of graphite, had written *we are he* in the southwest corner of the shape) and a network of thin, grey lines overlaid onto the map that showed him exactly how to get here.

His gaze shifted to the rectangular shape that looked like the church building.

Twenty-four.

Returning his attention to the monitors, he confirmed his suspicions and swallowed. On the corner of the screen with the tall glowing fish-tank-looking things, somebody had stuck the number *24*.

Answers.

His eyes moved from shape to shape, studying the map until he was sure. Until he was certain.

One or the other. Escape or answers.

He had a feeling he wouldn't get the chance to see both.

21

He moved slowly through the next corridor until it brought him to another door, this one shut firmly in the frame. Green lights winked above his head as he tried the handle – then, when he discovered it was locked, tried to kick it in. The door was solid, and he only succeeded in bruising the bottom of his foot. Cringing, he stumbled back and tried to remember the layout of the map on the wall. The door was arched and a circular window was set into it at his eye level, the glass reinforced by a grid of steel gauze. This was the way, he was sure of it.

Returning to the door, he leaned forward on his tiptoes and looked through the glass.

The window was smeared and greasy but beyond the door he could make out the vague shapes of an assortment of tables, the walls framed by *L*-shaped countertops. A refrigerator hung open beneath one of the counters, a flickering square of pale white light illuminating the bloodstained floor. Some kind of staff breakroom, he guessed, colourful plastic chairs scattered around the tables, a noticeboard on one wall covered in illegible post-its and grainy CCTV printouts. Cobwebs hung from the ceiling and a bank of flashing red lights was sunk into a smashed control panel on the opposite wall.

On the table nearest to him, the boy saw a half-full mug of coffee. The mug was bright red and though the design had begun to peel, he could discern the image of a cartoon giraffe with its neck snaking up the handle.

The coffee was still steaming.

The boy's eyes widened as he realised that the thin white wisps rising from the mug were more than just a smudge on the glass; someone had been in the breakroom recently.

There was someone else here.

He glanced back over his shoulder, desperately scanning the corridor for a door he'd missed, some kind of way around the breakroom that didn't involve going through – a ladder, maybe, a hatch in the ceiling that he could crawl through – or perhaps he could get underground again—

There was a scuffle the other side of the door like a chair leg scraping the floor and the boy winced, wheeling around to gaze wide-eyed through the window. His eyes flitted to the left as a tall shadow leered across the breakroom wall.

"Fuck," he whispered, recoiling from the door as the shadow sunk toward him. he staggered back and slammed his back against the corridor wall, dragging in a deep breath to flatten his stomach as sudden thumping footsteps loudened the other side of the door. There was a tinny, electronic beeping sound and then the *click* of a lock, and the boy held his breath tight in his throat as the door swung open.

Swallowing, he sunk back into the shadows as a shape appeared from inside the room and stepped out into the corridor. "Rissa?" the shape called, peering down the hall. She was tall: five-ten or so and Black, with thick dark hair and narrow cheeks. The boy was surprised to see that she wasn't dressed in the thick black body armour he'd assumed any of the thugs working here would wear; instead she wore a long, ragged white coat that was frayed at the hems and dark, grass-stained jeans. A pair of gold-rimmed eyeglasses hung around her slender neck on a delicate chain. "Rissa, is that you? I thought you were in the Big Room!"

She stepped past him, slipping her hands into her pockets and staring down the corridor. As quietly as he could, the boy reached up and gently ripped at the paper hospital gown's sleeve. It was sprayed with blood and sticky; as the scientist with the eyeglasses surveyed the hall, he reached cautiously around the door and pressed the fabric to the locking mechanism. It stuck, the half-congealed blood gluing it to rusted metal. He shrunk back as the scientist turned around.

"Fucking pipes," Eyeglasses murmured, turning around and storming back into the breakroom. Miraculously she didn't notice the boy lurking in the shadows behind the open door, instead reaching back blindly to grab it and slam it shut behind her.

He waited a moment before creeping back to the window and peering through.

For a minute the scientist fussed about the breakroom, shuffling papers on one of the countertops before stuffing them into a crisp manila folder. There was something written on the folder in marker pen, but before the boy could read it Eyeglasses had turned round and was marching back across the breakroom. He ducked back, sucking in another breath as she swung around the nearest table to grab her coffee.

After another minute, he looked again. Eyeglasses was gone; so was the coffee. A door across the room swung slowly shut after her. The folder lay closed on the countertop.

Gingerly, the boy reached for the handle and pulled.

The door opened with a *click* and the clump of fabric he'd left wedged around the lock-pin fluttered loose, falling to the floor at his feet. Quietly he stepped inside, keeping his eyes on the door through which Eyeglasses had disappeared.

The breakroom smelled of toast and nail varnish. He crossed it quickly, recalling the layout of the building and heading for the next door.

Halfway across the room, he paused. Glanced across at the manila folder.

Curiosity thumped in his throat.

His fingers were tucked into the folder before he could stop himself; he flicked it open and the cover gently slapped the countertop, knocking loose a small cloud of dust. Inside, a collection of papers and photographs had been pinned to official-looking files. He pored over the first document and saw that much of the text had been blotted out by thick strips of black, leaving only the words *Midlands* and *runoff* exposed in a sea of what looked like unravelled cassette-tape. Right at the bottom of the page, a handwritten footnote read *Just a few of us left now to carry on Arnett's work. Is this what he would have wanted?*

The boy shook his head, confused. Nudging the document aside, he revealed a sheet of notepaper beneath with another block of blacked-out text. At the top, a logo remained in faded red ink: it looked like a DNA double-helix inside a diamond-shaped block, only one of the interlocked DNA strands had been triplicated. The letters *MNCP* were printed in stencilled font beneath the logo.

Rifling through the rest of the papers he saw that most of them were entirely blacked-out, leaving only useless and unintelligible words and phrases uncensored. Annoyed, he turned instead to the photographs.

A bitter cold chill punched into his heart and spread through his entire body.

There were half a dozen images, each printed on a square of polaroid paper. The photographs were warped and taken at angles that made it difficult to discern exactly what was going on, but there was enough.

The first photograph had been taken at noon, with the sun a blot of bright white in one corner, and showed a small boy with sandy hair, five years old and clutching a half-eaten ice cream cone in one hand. There was chocolate all around his mouth and he was grinning. Behind the child, blurry shapes made up a rough approximation of a beachside scene; silhouettes loomed just out of sight, a huddle of them that could have been groynes as much as they could have been people.

In the next photograph, the child from the first was a little older. He stood in a pale jumper and jeans, staring straight at the camera with a man's hand on his shoulder. In this image, the child held a ragged teddy bear that looked more like a fuzzy porpoise with ears. The porpoise was in the third photograph, too: here the child sat on the carpet of a messy living room, playing peacefully among a collection of wildly-strewn toys while two adults sat on the floor behind him. One was a Black man with short, cropped hair and dark eyes, and the other a stocky woman in a summer dress.

In the next photograph, the subject of the photographs was seven or eight and playing with a toy plane while a blonde lady in a white coat stood behind him. Looking more closely, the boy saw that she was the same woman from the previous photograph.

In the last photograph, the Black man held the four-year-old boy in his arms, both of them smiling politely for the camera.

"What the fuck?" Brian Cooper whispered, looking into the eyes of the boy in the last photograph, bright and piercing though dashed with the distinctive red-eye of a cheap camera lens in poor lighting.

There was a whole childhood here, one that he could only assume had been documented in the accompanying files and then censored out of existence. Parents, he presumed: the Black man and the stocky woman. Gritty black-and-white images, snapshots from a happy, years-long life.

And though the childhood shown in these images wasn't anything like his own, the boy knew his own face. And there was no denying that the child in the photographs was him.

22

Teeth gritted, Brian Cooper passed into the next corridor and stalked the dark hall, keeping his head low, his back hunched so stiffly that the muscles of his shoulders and arms ached. He left a trail of blood and grit along the floor as he walked, his bare soles scraping the concrete. Dim multicoloured lights winked above him, spangles of red and green flaring among panels of beady purple and yellow. The underground humming of what he could only presume were large banks of machinery grew louder as he moved deeper into the building.

He was haunted by what he'd seen in the photographs, disturbed by the face of the child who looked so much like him. He wondered how old that other boy was now.

Did he have a twin? Had the burden of raising two children been too much for his parents, leading them to put one of the boys up for adoption? Perhaps the Black man and his scientist partner in the summer dress were foster parents.

Perhaps he had a brother out there that he'd never known about. An identical-looking young man who'd never grown up beneath the oppressive thumb of Brian Cooper's father, who'd never had to watch his mother take a belt to the leg or bear his own bruises either.

If he ever got out of here, the boy thought, he'd have to find him.

The prospect excited him a little as he moved slowly around a bend in the corridor, slowly traversing the mental map he'd extrapolated from the wall in the room with all the monitors. He had always felt lonely – even with Josh, and with the small circle of friends he'd managed to amass in his time at school – and perhaps it wasn't unreasonable to want one good thing to come out of this nightmare. Perhaps it was okay to be a little hopeful.

His mother had tried for another baby when the boy was ten years old. He remembered the jealous churlishness at first, a spitefulness in him that he couldn't control: it had lasted a few weeks from the moment she told him she was pregnant, only simmering to a hot paste when he saw how happy she had become. Then there was excitement, the prospect of a baby sister, a friend; company. Finally, when she was about ten weeks pregnant and her belly had started to swell, there was anguish: what if Brian's dad did the same to his sister that he'd done to Brian and his mother? What if she suffered, from the moment she was born to the day she moved out?

He didn't have to worry for too long. His mother miscarried at twelve weeks, the doctors attributing the strange and sudden loss of the baby to a severe haemorrhage in her abdomen. They suspected some kind of impact trauma, though when they asked her if she had fallen or experienced any other injuries, she told them nothing of the sort had occurred.

She wasn't the same when she returned from the hospital, but there was a relieved and wicked glint in Brian's father's eye that he had begun to recognise in recent years.

Swallowing as the memories stirred a sickening nest of hatred in his stomach, the boy turned another bend and stopped.

Fear pounded on his chest, begging to be let out.

At the end of the corridor, a figure in a long white coat stood scrawling something on a clipboard. She was shorter than the other scientist he had seen, and though her shoulders had narrowed a little he recognised her instantly from the photographs in the last room. He also had a faint suspicion that he knew her name: the Black lady with the eyeglasses and sallow cheeks had called it out as she stepped out of the breakroom.

Rissa.

She looked old, a good dozen years older than she had in the pictures. Perhaps more. Her hair was no longer thick and curled but pulled into a severe ponytail and greying at the temples. Her white coat was in better nick than the one Eyeglasses had worn; beneath it, she wore an Autumnal orange vest top and a baggy black skirt. Her tights were laddered and her shoes hadn't been polished in a while.

She stood absent-mindedly tapping the heel of one foot on the floor as she wrote; behind her were two doors, a pale circle of yellow light flickering through the window of the one on the right. A Walkman was tucked into the inside of her coat, the wires snaking up to a pair of bulky black headphones clamped over her ears. She hummed softly as she scribbled in her notepad.

Brian took a step back, and the woman looked up.

He froze as her eyes widened. His movement had been slight, slow, but enough to draw her attention: there was no doubt that she had seen them. Her lips parted slightly and he saw that the familiar eyes from those photographs had grown pale and rheumy, her cheeks and brow weathered with age. It was impossible: the boy in the photographs had been five or six, making them less than fifteen years old – that was, *if* the boy was Brian's twin and not some randomer that happened to look exactly like him – so how could she have aged so much? She looked at least twenty years older, maybe more.

Softly, she said, "Shit."

Then, as if remembering herself, the woman reached up to shove the headphones off her ears, one hand thrusting into her coat. She withdrew a clunky walkie-talkie with a long antenna and spoke frantically into it before the boy could run forward and stop her.

"All available staff, incursion in Factory Sector Eight. Repeat, all available staff—"

Realising what was happening, the boy rushed forward, lurching on his unsteady legs, opening his mouth to yell, to stop her. One scientist, he could deal with, but if she was calling backup…

"—incursion in Sector Eight. One full-formed. Urgent assistance required."

"Stop it," the boy snapped, swiping with one hand as he reached the end of the hall. Rissa backed up quickly, wheeling the walkie-talkie out of his reach. "Hey! Who are you calling? Who are you? What's going on here?"

Rissa recoiled, shaking her head as she stumbled backward for the nearest door. "You can't be in here," she whispered breathlessly. Raising the radio to her face again, she squawked impatiently: "Repeat, urgent assistance. One full-formed, Sector Eight. Can anyone hear me?"

"What does that mean?" the boy said, swiping for the radio again. His voice was hoarse and panicked. "What's a 'full-formed'? Where the hell am I?"

Ignoring him, she spoke into the walkie-talkie again. "Layla? Obie? Can anyone hear me? It… it can speak, and it's—"

Finally the boy managed to bat the radio out of her hand. It clattered the wall loudly and ricocheted onto the floor, skidding away from them as he loomed over her. Rissa backed into the door as his shadow fell across her face, fear filling her eyes. She scrabbled desperately for the handle as he spoke. "You tell me what the hell is going on here."

The scientist swallowed visibly, her fingers finally finding the handle. The boy tried to grab her but before he could knot his fingers into the lapel of her white coat she had shunted the door open and tumbled back through it. It slammed in his face and the boy hammered loudly on the steel, pounding with both fists as the dull *click* of a thrown bolt echoed in the corridor.

"Come on!" he yelled. "I just want some answers! I want to get out of here!"

The woman watched him through the glass, pale light blinking behind her. Her eyes flitted past him, to the walkie-talkie on the floor. Following her gaze the boy wheeled around, ducking down to grab it. He flexed his fingers around it and jabbed in a button on the side of the device, looking into Rissa's eyes as he spoke.

"Whoever's listening," he said into the radio, "I've had enough now. I want to get out of here, and I'm going to. You can send all the fucking severed hands and white coats after me that you like, I am *getting out of here*."

With that, he dropped the walkie-talkie onto the floor.

Rissa shook her head behind the glass, stepping back a pace. The boy fought with the handle for a moment before pounding on the door again. It didn't budge. Glancing over his shoulder, he looked toward the second door. Dark through the glass.

"They won't let you out, you know," Rissa said, her voice muffled.

He turned back to her. "Why?"

"They can't. You're not supposed to... well, you're not supposed to be here."

"You think I don't know that?"

"No, I mean... look, just leave me out of this. There's soldiers around this place. Not as many as there were, sure, but there's enough. And you've... where did you come from, underground? The compound? You've seen what *else* is out there."

The boy frowned. "Soldiers – the same ones who took me?"

Rissa hesitated. For a moment she looked confused, then her eyes flashed with realisation. "Who... who *took* you? Look, no, you've got it wrong; you're not—"

The loud *clap* of a door slamming down the hall stunned him and he wheeled around, staggering back as heavy, thumping footsteps started to echo into the corridor.

Soldiers.

"Fuck," the boy whispered, glancing in Rissa's direction before turning to the other door.

Down the corridor somebody yelled: "*Back against the wall, we will not hesitate to use lethal force!*" The heavy, pounding footsteps grew louder and the boy staggered back, moving shakily toward the door. He fumbled with the handle and it screamed open; tumbling through, he fell into a darkened room and turned around onto his back. Long shadows peeled onto the wall out in the corridor; panicking now, he heaved himself up and to the door, scrabbling for a bolt and slamming it across.

Something thick and heavy smashed into the door and he heard muffled yelling: "*Open that door! There's no way out through there, fuckhead!*"

Hyperventilating, the boy staggered backward, baulking as a stern white face appeared in the window. Night-vision goggles were pulled down over the figure's eyes and his teeth were gritted, a clipped haze of grey stubble chipping the icy structure of his cheeks. The door rattled again and the boy turned to run into the dark.

23

He crashed over a table and screamed as a bolt of agony ploughed into the flesh of his upper thigh. Behind him one of the soldiers continued to pound on the door, rhythmically slamming something heavy into the steel near the frame, trying to break it down.

The boy stumbled to the wall and followed it awkwardly until he reached the corner of the room, glancing back toward the door. Though most of the light from the corridor was obscured by the figure in the window, a little bled in and seeped in tones of grey across high, dust-coated workbenches and what looked like a messy assortment of scientific equipment. He glimpsed the splintered lens of a toppled microscope, a mismatch of beakers and flasks scattered across the worktop; thick spiral-bound notebooks and rubbery cables snaking over spatulas and rudimentary-looking medical supplies.

He was in a laboratory.

Moving along the next wall he fumbled for a door, his hip crying out as he bumped instead into another workbench. Struggling around it he ignored the pounding on the door behind him and the muffled yells of the soldiers – two of them, it sounded like – and half-jogged, half-stumbled into the next corner.

His hand found a rusted doorknob and he twisted, crashing through into another corridor. A motion sensor nearby must have been triggered by his movement: as he moved forward a long fluorescent strip of lighting came on above his head. Flickering but steady.

The map in his head was all turned around; cringing at the pain in his hip, the boy lurched forward and followed the corridor around to the right, where it split into an intersection. Three choices: left, right, or straight on. The fluorescent lighting in the hallway to his right was dim and the walls splashed with burnt, fizzing orange; he chose the left.

Way behind him now the door of the laboratory smashed open and the first soldier crashed into the room. The boy heard yelling and launched his tired legs into a run. His chest pounded, the thick fingers of a burgeoning stitch gripping his abdomen and twisting hard.

"*Move! Move!*" he heard behind him. One of the two soldiers cried into what the boy assumed was another radio: "*Incursion moving into Factory Sector Seven, all available units to the Nave!*"

Brian Cooper keened to a halt at the end of the corridor, faced with another pair of doors. This time there were faint lights behind both windows, all flickering and tinged with green. Quickly, adrenaline pumping through him like hot grease, he reached for the door on the right and yanked it open wide. Pivoting, he turned to the door on the left and wrestled it open, slipping through and closing it softly.

Panting, he pressed his back to the door and slid down, listening as the footsteps out in the corridor grew louder again. He squeezed his eyes shut and waited.

"Through here!" one of the soldiers called, kicking the right-hand door all the way open and stamping through into the next room. The boy let out a thick, hot breath of relief, his eyes snapping open – then he froze as a beam of bright white torchlight swung through the window above his head. He glanced up, watched as the second soldier shined his torch beam into the room. The soldier's face was grim and scarred down the left side, a crisscross of white tissue encircling a steel-grey eye.

"Coming," the second soldier muttered, his voice barely audible through the steel of the door.

The young man puffed air out of his cheeks and staggered to his feet.

Well, that was another minute or so he'd just bought for himself. He looked desperately about the room, scanning for a good way to use that time—

"Shit," he said as his gaze locked on the wide, blue eyes of a third soldier.

The man was tall, broad-shouldered, his hair jet-black and mussed. In one hand he held a damp paper cup, steam rising from the lip. A semi-automatic rifle swung lazily at his hip.

His mouth opened a little as he caught the boy's eye. Frowning, he slowly moved his free hand to his belt, fumbling for a familiar-looking radio device clipped there.

There was a soft *click* as he turned a dial, then the chirrup of the walkie-talkie coming online.

"Ah," the soldier said. He smiled thinly, shrugging in Brian Cooper's direction. "Wasn't turned on," he explained.

Slowly, almost cautiously, he reached back and set his coffee cup down. He raised both hands, not in surrender but something that looked like a show of good faith.

"You'd be Brian, then," the soldier said quietly.

The boy nodded. "Yes."

There was a long, taut silence that stretched between them. It snapped. "You're all so deluded," the soldier murmured, shaking his head – and then he grabbed the rifle at his belt with both hands and swung it up, punching back the trigger with a thick, gloved finger.

24

There was a burst of rifle-fire that sounded like a train rattling off the tracks.

The boy felt the heat before he registered any pain: a warm, almost pleasant bloom of wet heat spreading across his elbow. Then half a second later the pain hit all at once, a stream of empty ammunition shells sprinkling the floor as a million electrical signals fired all along his right forearm. It was like somebody had shoved his hand and wrist into a blender and the blades were spinning at the speed of sound; one moment there was that sickly sweet warmth, and the next there was a bright, brilliant surge of agony like nothing he'd ever felt before.

He yowled as his arm exploded, his whole body launched back into the wall. Somewhere in the factory he heard yelling. The other soldiers, alerted to his location by the gunfire. The boy's elbow was twisted back and the force of the impacts screaming through his forearm one after the other seemed to have dislocated his shoulder.

When the bullets had stopped punching through his bone and muscle and smacking the wall behind him, the boy looked down.

His arm was gone from the elbow down. The elbow itself was a ragged knot of gooey cartilage, thick threads of blood oozing down from the nub. The floor and wall behind him were splashed with chunks of metal and bone and muscle, flesh ripped to ribbons. He thought he could see a curled finger sitting in a thick gob of red meat. It took him a second to realise that the screaming in his ears was his own; his voice seemed to dry up suddenly as he looked in the soldier's direction. Agony sheared his upper arm and chest. "What the fuck?!" he yelled.

The soldier frowned, slamming a new clip into the rifle. "Sorry about that," he muttered, "haven't had to fire this boy off in a while."

With that he swung the rifle upward again.

The young man's eyes went wide and he ducked as another spray of bullets punched through the air, slamming into the wall as they separated the air where his head had been. "Jesus!" he yelled, mania firing up again in his veins. He knew his body should be shutting down: his arm had been entirely severed at the elbow and the agony was ripping his whole right side apart; he felt woozy and drained – but a thick forceful wave of adrenaline ploughed him forward.

The other side of the room the soldier swore, swinging the gun around to follow the now-moving target surging toward him. "I'm gonna shoot you in the fucking face, cunt!" he yelled through gritted teeth.

The boy ducked to one side as another barrage of gunfire filled the room. Something hot and bright clipped his left shoulder and he howled, barrelling forward and launching himself at the soldier. His whole weight – now a good few pounds lighter than it had been before, even in its malnourished state – managed to knock the tall man back a couple feet and Brian Cooper yelled, wrapping the soldier in an awkward one-armed bear hug. "Fuck you!" he yelled.

The two of them crashed into a low worktop and the boy heard glass breaking. More beakers sprayed the floor, shattering into sharp icy chips. The bulky rifle slammed into the boy's side and he grunted, staggering back, his mutilated elbow winging blood and viscera.

The boy's face flashed with darkness and he launched himself forward again, screaming with anger and pain as the soldier raised the semi-automatic, pointing the chunky black barrel right between his eyes—

He smashed his body into the soldier's arm just as the man squeezed the trigger. The gun swung up – *up* – and an explosion of meat and bone sprayed the ceiling with red as a torrent of bullets passed cleanly through the soldier's chin, brain, and skull. His scalp burst open in a thick red mist and his eyes rolled up, then filled suddenly and violently with red.

The boy screamed and tumbled into the workshop as the soldier's body went limp and crumpled onto its knees.

"What the fuck?!" the young man yelled. "*Jesus shitting Christ, what the fuck?!*"

The soldier's body toppled backward, its ruined head – little more than a bulging sac of pink flesh and shattered bone – flopping onto its back. The gun crashed to the floor.

Behind them, the door slammed open.

"*Fu—uck!*" the boy roared, stumbling to his feet and lurching across the room toward the next door. There was another eruption of booming gunfire and he screamed as he yanked the door open and rolled through, bullets smacking the glass behind him.

Clutching his savaged elbow, he looked up and saw that he'd wound up in another corridor. Without the time to think or try and process the map he'd half-memorised, now turned over and over in his head and split in half by the nausea in his gut and the pain quickly eroding the remnants of his arm, he ran.

A spray of bullets hit the wall as he flung his body around a corner and into another door. Green lights flashed above his head, strips of fluorescent white buzzing erratically in steel rivulets in the walls. A whirlwind of agonised howling surged at the back of his skull and he barrelled into the wall, the corridor swimming and yawing open before him as he staggered forward. He managed to crash through another door and bolted it awkwardly behind him, dragging his body through what might have been a cloakroom: it looked like it hadn't been used in years, with many of the white coats hung up on long rails now covered in thick clumps of cobweb. Into another corridor, round to the left; slamming and locking another door, his skull a hunk of wood chainsawed in half then clapped together again and again and again—

He stopped in a long, red-lit corridor, fingers squeezing the flesh above his ruined elbow. Blood swung from the wounded nub in thick red threads, pattering the floor at his feet.

Strips of tiny, round lights hammered into the walls flickered and thrummed in unison. Some of the lights were dim white, some filtered blood-red. The effect was a wash of pinkish, fluid afterglow.

The boy staggered forward, toward a door at the very end of the corridor. This one wasn't like the others: it was tall, arched, the frame and the surrounding wall made of chipped limestone and flint. The door itself was a heavy wooden thing, polished black hinges bleeding into prominent, ornately-welded designs along its edge. The handle was the head of a grinning wild animal, its teeth bared.

This was it.

The point where the twisted labyrinth of the factory fused with the original architecture of the old church.

Storming forward, the young man laid his good hand on the doorknob with the smashed teeth and twisted.

25

The church might once have been a grand spectacle of lime and gargantuan carved archways, but now it was threaded with gridded knots of iron pipework and thick black cables; the factory behind him had funnelled into the ancient building and slapped panels and banks of steel onto the stone walls, mutilating the architecture in a brutal wave of grey-black. long tendrils of electrical wiring snaked up the arches looming over the nave, and thick bunches of ivy surged up through cracks in the brickwork and clung to bulging metal pillars. As he stepped forward he was splashed with a multicoloured assault of glowing lights; his eyes flitted from enormous banks of machinery to the stained-glass windows behind them and he saw that many of those windows remained intact, the awful scenes depicted in shards of red and gold filtering moonlight into vast spangles of brilliantly ghoulish purple that lay over the flagstones.

The pews had been removed and the great open space that remained had been filled with tanks. There must have been three dozen of them altogether, tall wide pillars of glass encased in thick concrete brackets, each one twice the height and three times the width of a man. Cylinders of glittering emerald, all filled with a fluid that seemed to bubble and thrash behind the glass. The boy moved deeper into the church building and peered at the nearest tank: the glass was frosted – evidently the contents were being kept at an immensely low temperature, and now he realised that he could feel the cold in the air, too, seeping out from the pillars and spreading all around him – and it was impossible to see anything inside but vague washes of colour.

Nonetheless, he thought he could make out dark shapes twitching and writhing in each tank, suspended in the bubbling green fluid.

"What the…"

He waded through the cold and lurched forward, blood dripping slowly from his wasted elbow. The pain hadn't subsided, but his confusion and the mania burning him up were frazzling his nerve endings so harshly that he had no reliable gauge for how much he hurt.

Gradually the young man stalked forward, falling into the shadow of the huge tank closest to him. The flags beneath him were worn, each stone smoothed into a shallow pit where it had been knelt upon over centuries; crusty dark stains spattered the walls and many of the cracked cement slabs at his feet. Across from him, barely visible between two rows of green-glowing tanks, was a tall stained-glass window depicting the archangel Michael slaying a beastly, red-tongued creature that might have been the Devil. Beside Michael, a woman in a pale blue hood was reciting from a heavy book.

As the boy reached the nearest tank he looked up, awed by the sheer cold radiating from it. The glass was pebbled and a good two or three inches thick, riveted halfway up and then at regular intervals with thick clunky bands of iron. Now that his senses had cooled he could hear the soft bubbling all around him, muffled by the glass and almost drowned out by the constant, pneumatic hissing of the tanks. Beneath the floor there was a low, persistent droning that he'd been able to ignore so far; now, looking down, he saw that he was stood among a nest of snakelike cables that exploded from the base of each cylindrical tank and shot out into the walls.

Behind a thick coating of frost, the shape in the tank convulsed. It was alive, he realised with a sick churning in his gut. About the size and shape of a man, though he couldn't see in enough detail to discern any more than that.

Gingerly, Brian Cooper reached out to lay his hand on the glass. It was freezing, and an eerie ring of vibration pulsed into his palm. Inside, the writhing creature seemed to respond, vague shapes that might have been hands clenching into tight balls.

"What are you?" he whispered.

Somewhere in the church a door slammed shut. He hadn't heard it open; furtively he glanced back over his shoulder to see that the door he'd come in through was still ajar.

Quietly he backed away from the tank, the agony in his arm suddenly surging through him again. He could almost still feel the fingers twitching but when he tried to close his fist there was nothing there and a bolt of pain shot across the stump of his elbow.

"Who's there?" he called, immediately regretting it.

Across the church, somewhere behind the farthest bubbling fish-tanks, sharp heels clicked tentatively on the flagstones. These weren't the thumping steps of the soldiers.

"I've got a gun," he lied, "I took it from one of the guards. I know how it works."

"You haven't," called a soft female voice, "you didn't – and you don't."

More footsteps in the corridor behind him. He wheeled around to look through the open door but saw nobody there. Terrified he padded into the labyrinth of tanks, slipping between two giant green cylinders and ducking behind another. At the other end of the church building, another door screamed open and snapped shut. Christ, how many fucking doors were there?

"Who are you?" the young man said loudly, the echo of his voice booming off the glass tubes around him. His face and bare skin were bathed in a swimming green hue and he dripped a steady trail of blood onto the flags. The hospital gown hung in ragged strips across his mutilated body. He shivered in the intense cold enveloping him.

"I don't think that's the right question, is it?" came the woman's voice again, this time from somewhere behind him. "Who are *we*? That's not what you really want to know."

"Nancy," hissed another voice, somewhere off to his right. "Shut up."

He vaguely recognised the voice as Rissa's, though it was difficult to tell. The last time he'd seen her – minutes ago, though it felt like an eternity had passed (he supposed that feeling was reasonable, since his arm had been shot off his body) – she hadn't wanted to get anywhere near him. Why was she here now? Had she led the guards right to him?

The first woman spoke again, and as the boy turned his head to look in the direction of her voice he saw that it was the narrow, Black scientist with the eyeglasses that he'd seen before. "Ask me another question," she called, her eyes skipping from one glass canister to the next.

Brian Cooper glanced through a funnel of green glass toward a door at the end of the church. Escape. But he couldn't just dart for it, not yet. She was right. He needed to know.

"Who are *they*?" he tried. "The people in the tanks."

He almost heard the smile in her voice: "That's better."

"Nancy!" Rissa hissed again, somewhere in front of him now. They were circling him – carefully scanning the rows of tanks, he realised, looking for him – and he slunk around the nearest to pad quietly through the maze.

Eyeglasses spoke cruelly, as if she were enjoying all of this. "They," she said, "are—"

"*Nancy!*"

The boy swallowed, looking up into the cylinder looming above him. Inside it, a burry but decidedly human shape looked back out.

"Tell me," he called, moving again so that he'd be elsewhere by the time they pinpointed the source of his voice. "Tell me who they are."

"They," she said slowly, "are Brian Cooper."

26

The frightened nineteen-year-old froze stock still and his blood seemed to stop pumping through his body. Beside him, a shadowy figure wriggled violently behind a thick wall of frosted glass. Bubbles thrashed on the surface of the encased green fluid high above him.

"Say that again," he whispered.

"Brian Cooper," Nancy said, seemingly right behind him now. He pivoted on his heel, peering into the banks of gently-pulsating containers. Nobody there. The woman cleared her throat. "Arnett looked everywhere for a reasonable specimen. The project required somebody with very… specific physical attributes. Nothing out of the ordinary, but quite specific. Blood type, body mass index, exact percentage of healthy cells… like I say, he looked *everywhere*. He found a boy called Brian."

"Who's Arnett?" the boy called, stumbling past a tank toward a tall stained-glass window upon which was a fractured image of a long, green snake coiled around a thick red-barked trunk. As he moved his elbow slapped one of the tanks and left a sloppy blood-red smudge. "What the hell project are you talking about?"

Far behind him now, the scientist's voice continued. "A boy called Brian Cooper. Nothing special, just… right. And his parents were willing to donate him."

The young man blinked. Looking to the left, he caught a glimpse of a shadow flitting between the tanks. *Rissa.* He wasn't safe in here anymore, had to get out into the open. Had to get closer to that door.

"I remember being taken," the boy called, staggering into the nearest tank and half-bouncing off, his legs entangling each other as the adrenaline started to wear off. "They came for me in the library…"

"They came for *Brian Cooper* in the library," one of the scientists said. The voice was different: Rissa's. She seemed significantly less thrilled to be telling this story. "At any rate, his parents told Arnett where to find him."

"This isn't true," he protested. A thick wedge of moonlight struck him and he stumbled deeper into it, almost falling into the nave.

"I think Carl Cooper was reasonably satisfied with the amount of money Arnett offered."

"Who's *Arnett*?!" the boy almost screamed.

"Even Brian's mother seemed to abandon any qualms she may have had when she saw the amount they were receiving for their… very generous donation."

He shut his eyes, crumpling onto his knees. Pain rippled through his upper body.

A hand clapped down on his shoulder. He didn't look up, didn't open his eyes. Softly, her voice coming from somewhere just beyond his left side, Rissa whispered, "I'm sorry."

Nancy's voice was closer now, too. "Any more questions before we dispose of you?"

The boy shook his head. Slumping forward, he struggled weakly out of Rissa's grasp. To his surprise, she let him; he slopped awkwardly onto his feet and turned around, backing away from her. He got the best look at her that he'd been granted so far, and finally he saw the years in her eyes. The sorrow.

His eyes dropped to the gun in Rissa's hand.

A thin shape emerged from the row of tanks nearest to them, and the boy swallowed as Nancy stepped forward, her own eyes alight with green flames. "Do you understand what they are, now?" she said. "The

127

things in the tanks? Do you understand what *you* are?"

The boy looked from Rissa to Nancy and blinked. "I don't understand *shit*," he said, gluey saliva bubbling weakly over his bottom lip. "What the fuck was any of that?"

Rissa smiled kindly, her face wrinkled with sadness. "Clones," she said simply. "They're clones."

27

Nancy Hammond raised a slender, long-fingered hand to the nearest tank and swiped away a layer of frost. Behind the glass a dimly-lit face flashed its teeth, eyes closed. Sleeping fitfully in the container.

"The boy was taken in the summer of 1990," she said calmly, looking up into the tank. "Arnett sent men to collect him, making sure they knew to leave him unharmed. He was brought to the facility – much smaller back then, but busier. We used to have a staff of more than a hundred, you know. Not many of us left, now. The project grew... complicated. Arnett died, of course. Only a few of us were willing to stay and finish his work.

"Imagine it: duplicating a body entirely, artificially manifesting exact organic replicas—"

There was an emphasis on each of those words: *Exact. Organic. Replicas.*

"—from a healthy base template. There are plenty of examples of semi-successful cloning, of course, but Arnett wanted to perfect the craft. The military application was – still is – astounding."

Rissa grappled uncomfortably with the small pistol in her hand, flexing her fingers as Nancy spoke. Her eyes never left the boy's face.

"He wanted to go a step further, too. You're picturing, I hope, an army of identical soldiers, as many of them as you desire, each one created not through unpredictable biological processes but via a systematic, pressurised, *reliable* scientific operation. You're picturing an army of Brian Cooper. Disposable fodder, perhaps. Valuable in their own right."

"I don't understand," the boy whispered. "You cloned me?"

Nancy smiled thinly, finally turning to him. "More than that. Like I said, Arnett wanted to go a step further than successful cloning. Imagine the value of an assembly-line army. A supply of new soldiers limited only by the funds of whoever wished to deploy them. Fine. But… why not go one better?

"So Arnett set us to work on crafting a healing genome. On inseminating into these clones the ability to reproduce appendages over time – to heal potentially fatal wounds within hours, minor ones in minutes."

"This doesn't make any sense."

"No? Well, then imagine you've spent a certain amount of money on an army of identical soldiers. Now, imagine half of them die. Another thirty per cent lose limbs; the rest might be fine, but with continued use, the same will happen to them, too. You might win one battle, or a war if you're lucky, but if your men can still die, then at the end of it all…"

"Your money's gone, and you've got nothing to show for it," Rissa said, her eyes rheumy and vacant. "Those were Arnett's words."

"Sounds like a real gent," the young man said bitterly, pain rocking his body on its weary feet.

"But if those soldiers could heal – could repair their bodies at a capacity greater than humanly possible… well, then, you've got an infinite supply. Your fatally-wounded soldiers would be ready to go by the time another battle comes along. Your soldier who's lost a hand and can't shoot anymore – what do you know, in minutes he's grown back his hand and he's eager for another go at the trigger."

"Seems like a bad business model," the boy choked, "what about all your return customers?"

"We didn't just do this for the military," Nancy snapped. "We did this for science."

He looked past her, at the vague shapes swimming in their tanks, and swallowed. "You actually... this is bullshit. They don't even look like me."

"It's true," Rissa whispered.

"But... I woke up a few hours ago. Before that, I was in the library. You're talking about 1990 like it's in the past. But I... I mean, how long was I asleep? A day or two?"

"You weren't asleep," Rissa said. "Until today, you've never technically been awake."

Nancy smiled cruelly. "It's 2023, *Brian*."

28

It wasn't real. It couldn't be. The more he heard the more convinced he became that they were lying: even if the science behind all this were possible, there was no way any government would be fucked enough to let this kind of work continue. And if it were all done underground, then where did the funding come from?

They were lying. They had to be.

The taller of the two women winced suddenly, as if disgusted by the young man standing before them. She reached up and plucked the eyeglasses off her nose, tucking them into her coat. "I think we've explained enough. Get rid of him."

Beside her, Rissa opened her mouth as if to protest. The gun in her hand was trembling.

"Is there a problem?" Nancy said. "Go on. Just shoot him and take him to the incinerator."

"Wait!" the boy yelled, raising his good hand. His eyes flitted to the nearby door. Back again. "I don't... I don't get it. Shoot me. Fine. I've pretty much accepted I'm not getting out of here. But fill me in, at least. You don't get to do this very often, right? Not many people to talk to around here, I don't think. And you'd never be able to gloat about all this work to someone you *weren't* going to shoot. Am I right?"

Nancy cocked an eyebrow.

"I don't get it," the boy said honestly, looking from one scientist to the other and back again. "When I woke up, I was underground. There were... things, down there. And a hand – out in the corridor – it attacked me. And I want to get this straight in my head. I want to know..."

I want to know if you're lying to me. If I'm a clone, or if I'm the real Brian Cooper.

"What am I, if I'm not him?"

"Let's revisit the soldier who got his hand shot off, shall we?" Nancy said, folding her arms. "See if you can follow this."

"I'm listening." The young man glanced down at the gun in Rissa's hand.

"Growing back entire limbs isn't easy," Nancy said. "It shouldn't be possible. And there's no way I could explain the science to you. Let's just say... I'll tell you what, let's say that every single cell in the clone's body was imbued with a certain level of sentience. I suppose we could call it biological intelligence. Each cell's mental capacity – if you could call it that, even – would be limited to what it needed in order to regrow. To reform. But it would still have *a* capacity."

"Right."

"A few minutes pass. The cloned soldier starts to regrow his hand. Bones, muscles, tendons all start to form, to fuse together. Within an hour, he's whole again. Understood?"

He did understand – or had started to, anyway. "So what happens to the hand?" he whispered.

"*There* we are," Nancy said quietly. "You got there in the end."

"Okay," the boy shook his head. "So the hand starts to regrow an arm. And maybe it takes a bit longer, but eventually it's grown a whole extra body. Am I right? The cell-intelligence – or whatever – doesn't just exist in the original body. It can't. It's also there in any part of the body that's removed."

"Ex-*actly*."

"You cut one of these clones in half, and eventually you get two."

"Cut them into ten," Rissa said weakly, "and you get... well, as many as you like."

"An infinite supply of soldiers," Nancy breathed. "Imagine."

The boy swallowed. "But it doesn't quite work like that, right? You said it yourself: that intelligence is limited. You're talking about this like it's been successful, but—"

"We're working on it," Nancy said curtly.

"The things I saw underground... in the room where I woke up... organs all smashed together. Lungs on top of lungs. Hands and intestines all fused into some weird fucking... I don't know. Some kind of *creature*."

"Individual organs trying to regrow," Nancy explained. "They don't always get it right."

"So everything down there is just... a reject?"

"Periodically, we bring everything above ground to be incinerated," Nancy said casually. "But you have to understand that even a single cell can regrow with enough time."

"It's endless," Rissa added, her eyes on the floor. The gun, he noticed, was finally still in her hand.

"So what am I?" the boy whispered. "Just a lopped-off hand that had a few hours to spare?"

"Something like that."

He remembered something else. Another detail. Down in the basement, the hospital gowns all hung on the wall. A dozen or so of them. "I'm not the first, am I?" He looked at Rissa. "When you called the guards, you said there was an incursion. A *full-formed*. Is that all I am?"

Nancy answered. "Outside – you may have seen them – there are many. Most of them not quite fully formed. *Skin* seems to be difficult, oddly. Ninety-nine per cent of the discarded organs or parts which are allowed to regrow to that extent gain an amount of intelligence, but never quite attain human levels. They look... off. And they're fairly weak."

"So I'm a rarity," the boy said bitterly.

"Quite. But proof, I think, that the science *can* work."

"And you're going to shoot and burn me?"

"Yes."

"Why? If I'm proof that—"

"Because you fuck things up. You, and others like you." Her eyes narrowed. "You always *fuck things up*."

He nodded. Looked one last time at the tanks. Three-dozen Brian Coopers hung lazily in the air, suspended in eerily-glowing fluid.

"Fine," he said, closing his eyes. Agony burned his right side. His whole body ached for this to be over. And now his mind was in ruins. Was all of this real? Was *any* of it? "Get it done."

A brief pause, in which he almost felt the scientists glancing at each other and, finally, coming to a decision.

"It's been nice talking to you," Nancy said flatly.

There was a titanic *clap* as the barrel of the gun in Rissa's hand exploded.

29

Something warm splashed his face and he drew in a sharp intake of breath, expecting perhaps half a second of unbridled agony before all the lights went out.

After a moment, his eyelids snapped up on crusty hinges. There was no pain, save for the intense and constantly blossoming aches up his arm and into his chest. No blackness except the clouds of it that swum at the edges of his vision.

He was alive.

A few feet from him, Nancy gargled blood.

His eyes moved from the smouldering gun in Rissa's hand to the taller, Black woman standing next to her. The breath trapped at the back of his throat was expelled as he let a dismayed moan slip out of his mouth.

Nancy swayed for a moment on her feet, one side of her face punctured with a deep, inch-thick black hole that drizzled slowly down her neck. The other side had exploded outward where the mangled bullet had punched out through her cranium, withdrawing chunks and ribbons of brain matter as it flew into a looming limestone archway. Tiny dots of white stone flecked the floor where they had blown loose; behind the woman, a small spattering of gore clung to the frosty outer wall of a tall green tank, minute specks of meat already burning with

136

the extreme drop in temperature.

Nancy's eyes were wide, one of them filled with red. Slowly, she turned her head to look at Rissa. Her lips parted as though she were about to question the older woman.

Instead, she fell. Her knees crumpled and her head lolled forward, and then she was lying in a limp mess at the boy's feet, blood pooling slowly from her opened skull.

The young man looked at Rissa.

She was weeping softly, the gun trembling in a shaking hand. Her eyes were wet with sorrow. "You have to go," she choked, evidently finding it difficult to talk; her voice was hoarse and cracked with emotion. She gestured with the gun, pointing vaguely in the direction of the door through which Nancy had entered. "Get out of here. Get as far as you can."

Brian Cooper shook his head. "Why?"

Smiling sadly, Rissa looked at him with something like recognition. He understood the moment before she told him: "I raised you. Another you. One of the first clones. They needed to test the boy's development in a normal environment."

"The photos…"

She nodded, reaching up to wipe away a tear. "You were a good boy," she whispered. "Please… go. Now. You might make it out of here if you run."

"Thank you," the boy said, his throat tight.

"*Go.*"

He lurched past her toward the door, trying desperately to ignore the desperate, watchful eyes of the vague figures in the cylindrical fish-tanks. He could feel them through inches of glass, feel them on his back…

They weren't him.

They couldn't be.

30

The door slammed behind him and he staggered out into the night, a sharp assault of cold air ploughing into his body. In the shadow of the church building he looked desperately around him: tall patches of grass lunged at the feet of crooked stone crosses and chipped headstones; thick clumps of moss dressed the stone, blue and fuzzy in the moonlight. A thin dirt path wound through the cemetery and downhill toward a tall iron fence, beyond which he could just make out the faint silhouettes of ramshackle buildings. The path was mostly overgrown and damp weeds bent into the dirt and tangled around each other's throats, strangling and oppressive.

He took a few swaying steps forward and froze as the *smack* of another gunshot boomed behind him, echoing inside the church building.

"No…" he moaned, a twisted knot of guilt tightening as the cruel hands of despair and sorrow tugged the ropes inside his stomach.

Don't look back. Don't think about it.

The church was on the crest of a steep, black slope, every part of the incline thick with ragged black matter. He looked to the right, past the abandoned village below and into the dark, and saw faraway lights, blinking orange. A gaseous cloud of amber seeped into the night air above what he hoped was a small town; farther around to the right, separated from that town by a scar of black horizon, was another cluster of paler, dimmer lights. It would be a hell of a walk, but there was civilisation.

His eyes dropped. At the foot of the hill he saw a leaning structure that at first looked like a skeletal windmill; as he squinted into the dark he realised it was a watchtower of some kind. Beyond the whooping of the wind as it slunk through the cemetery grounds, he heard low voices. More soldiers.

It's not real. None of it's real.

"I am Brian Cooper," he insisted to himself, his own voice broken and fragile. None of what Nancy had said was true; it couldn't be. He *remembered* being taken from the library, and nothing in between… he hadn't been here more than a few days. Couldn't have been. After all, he'd not *seen* the faces of the things in those tanks, not in detail… and the things underground… well, whatever sick kind of science they were doing here, it wasn't him. Couldn't be. Couldn't be. *Couldn't* be.

None of it's real.

Except the guns. The guards, the soldiers; *they* were real.

Brian Cooper or not, the boy had to be careful.

He lurched forward, escaping the shadow of the church and shivering as the cool, damp fingers of the grassy earth knotted around his ankles. His bare feet pressed into malnourished earth and he relished the soft-by-comparison sensation of something non-concrete, something organic. His legs were sore, his upper body worse. Never mind finding a telephone, his first call had to be locating a hospital. Somewhere in those clustered banks of light on the horizon, there had to be something…

He moved slowly, stumbling around the corner of the church and glancing up as he ventured deeper into the graveyard. The building's spire loomed high above him, deep red lights glaring through tiny windows. Behind it, the enormous bulk of what must have been the factory's hub rose up in a solid mass of moonlit grey: a gargantuan cylinder of steel with ladders running all the way up to the top, a network of tunnels and corridors feeding into it from the church and the labyrinth of smaller structures surrounding it.

The young man padded cautiously through the cemetery and returned his attention to the horizon. There were more watchtowers at the foot of the hill, four that he could see, spread out at intervals. Each one manned, presumably, though he knew they were operating with a skeleton crew. If he approached each one carefully, listened for signs of occupation, if he slipped out now, in the dark, while he could…

Something grumbled wetly a few feet from him.

He looked in the direction of the sound, his heartbeat spiking. It was a low, guttural moan, sloppy and gargling, muffled by layers of earth. The boy's eyes traversed spiked headstones and crooked, cracked slabs and he moved slowly forward, creeping between the graves. His gaze was focused on a patch of short, clipped grass among the thready clumps of longer, unkempt plant matter. A faint glint of moonlight on metal. Shoulder throbbing painfully, he held his breath and stepped closer.

The sound again: a quiet, deep gurgle. One he recognised.

Swallowing, he stepped up to the manhole cover and looked down into the earth.

The lid had been shunted aside and he could see all the way down into the sewer through a ragged hole in the grass. A mangled ladder rutted out of the cement funnel, a thick sloppy current of red and yellow running far below.

Organs climbed the walls toward him.

His eyes widened with horror as he saw dreadful shapes clinging to the cement, slopping and heaving their way up through the earth. A stretched, brown liver suckered to one of the rungs of the ladder flipped its weight upward, latching on to the next rung and quivering as it did so. A slab of striated muscle with a spine dangling from it like a tail seemed to be crawling upward, the connected vertebrae swinging behind it as it moved. Gloopy red chunks dragged themselves up the walls, half-spherical clumps of translucent yellow the size of baseballs carving a pus-slick path between deformed lungs and snakelike, slithering tendons.

140

Panicking, the boy lurched down to grab the manhole cover. It was lying a few inches from the hall and half-buried in the earth; clearly something had come up through the very same hole some time ago, leaving it open. He fumbled, struggling to grab the cover with his good hand, momentarily forgetting that he'd lost the other – his stump cried out painfully as he worked the shoulder of the useless arm – and slipped, crashing onto one knee.

Beneath him, wet slops and gargles echoed up the funnel of the earth.

"Oh, no, you don't," the boy muttered through gritted teeth, grabbing the lid like a frisbee and heaving it out of the earth. Dirt flew and he swayed on his knee, swiping the manhole cover awkwardly into place. "There—"

As he wrestled with the thing a thick, blood-red tendon snapped up out of the hole and lashed his wrist, whipping back before he could react. A bulging mass of yellowish kidney and stomach, fused into a globular cone of raw wet viscera, squeezed out through the gap before he could close it fully, its awful membrane stretching as it reached for him hungrily. The boy yowled, slamming the manhole cover into the abomination with a wet hiss before punching the lid down and stamping it into the earth.

Backing away from the cover, he stumbled into a hunk of chipped stone, grazing the back of his calf. He yelped, wheeling around, almost tripping over a shattered branch at his heels.

Shouting voices from the edge of the churchyard. Somewhere a shining arc of white light swept up and spotted the church wall.

"Shit," the boy hissed, ducking low. With his good hand he gripped the top of the headstone to keep himself upright. His eyes slid to the name imprinted on the stone, carved a quarter of an inch deep in tall, imperial font:

Brian Cooper

He blinked. His head shot up as thumping footsteps pounded the grass behind the church. More guards. Somewhere off to his left, he heard a low, rasping grunting sound. More half-formed monstrosities from below ground?

Ignoring the sounds he crawled forward, swiping a clump of moss from the face of the next headstone, a narrow obelisk of crumbling grey-white. A knot of fuzzy black fell through his fingers and the faded lettering became visible:

Brian Cooper

Nothing else – no dates, no details – just a name. His name.

Whipping his head around he scanned the headstones across from him, a row of three crosses slanting out of the ground.

Brian Cooper

Brian Cooper

Brian Cooper

"No," he moaned, stumbling to his feet. "No…"

It wasn't real. Couldn't be. He threaded the fingers of his remaining hand into his hair and twisted, heart pounding too fast. Turning at another low rasp from behind him he saw awful white-skinned figures slinking toward him between the headstones, some of them ripped in half with their organs spilling into their pale, long-fingered hands, some of them missing heads, or missing legs and dragging themselves through the grass by their smooth, flat fingers…

"Shit. No. No, no, no…"

He staggered backward, looking left and right. Soldiers in the field below him to the left, three or four of them sweeping torchlights back and forth across the headstones.

"*Shit…*"

He turned, stumbling back toward the church. His eye caught another stone as he passed between them

Brian Cooper

and he baulked, nausea roiling in his mouth. His head was swimming.

A red-raw hand swiped at his face and he screamed, ducking beneath short stubby fingers and tumbling into another obelisk. His attention was stolen by the name on the stone as the claws of a

Brian Cooper

stumpy dead little ash tree scratched his neck.

"You! Hold it there!" yelled a harsh feminine voice and he heard the deafening *clack-clack* of a rifle cocking. Torchlight blinded him and he ducked, smashing his wounded arm into another gravestone and oozing red fluid across the

Brian Cooper

carved there.

"It's not real," he muttered to himself, ducking into the deep grass and launching himself between a pair of leaning black angels, their faces blank and emotionless. A spray of gunfire smacked the air like rain falling all at once. Something nicked the back of his leg and he kept running, forcing himself toward the back of the church, toward the long shadow of the spire and the thick black pillar of industrial madness lurking behind it. "It's not real, can't be, can't be real can't be real notrealnotrealnotreal—"

He howled as smooth fingers knotted into his hair and yanked back his head. Lashing out with a bare, aching foot he slammed his weight back into the creature and turned, watching it stumble back into the gravestones. Its face was gone, its torso open so that he could see the mess inside its chest. Two hearts pumped in rhythm, fused together at the ventricles, working to inflate and compress a single black lung. Yellow fluid spilled from the cavity. Behind the first creature a second heaved itself forward on a single thick, trunk-like leg, veins running through white skin, toes and fingers poking out of the knee and calf like tumours.

"Fuck off!" he yelled, careening backward.

BrianCooperBrianCooperBrianCooper

A siren somewhere. More voices:

"Rogue unit heading for the Big Room, I repeat, rogue unit heading for the—"

"—eyes on the target, fire!"

Instinctively he ducked. Bullets smashed through the white, featureless skull of the first creature and punched chunks from the church wall behind him. He swung his body to the right and ducked beneath another swinging arm, this one twisted and dripping great strings of blood. A pale creature hissed as he rammed his shoulder into its torso and somewhere behind him another guard flung her rifle forward, squeezing the trigger and letting loose a barrage of shot. The air was suddenly hot and electric and smelled like a bonfire.

"Stay the fuck still!"

He decided to ignore that advice and barrelled forward, tumbling into the shadow of the massive steel funnel behind the church. It filled the entire sky above him, blotting out all the moonlight, parts of it scratched and pocked with rivets. A ring of bleeding blue lights at the top blinked on and off, replaced seconds later with a series of dim red flashes.

Not real. It's a lie. I am Brian Cooper.

They had cloned him. Fine. Messed with the clones beyond all hope, created those abominations downstairs... okay. Okay, maybe that was real.

But he wasn't one of them. He was the real Brian Cooper, and he had the memories to prove it.

Maybe they all do.

"No!" he screamed, burning hot pain searing his hip as a bullet sheared his flesh, another spray of them disappearing into the burnt darkness in front of him. "I'm real! I'm fucking real, leave me alone!"

He swayed drunkenly forward, heading for a ladder knotted into the wall of the factory building. Behind him, six or seven torchlights swung in his direction. Another half-dozen off to his left, and more spreading all around the churchyard. He sensed movement to his right and saw more of those awful half-formed creatures coming up from the ghost town below, some of them crawling up the walls of the church, leaving sloppy gelatinous trails on the stone.

A torch beam knifed through the rungs of the ladder and three more soldiers appeared, visors covering their faces, not a single inch of skin exposed to the night. The guns they carried were long and bulky – Jesus Christ, flamethrowers? – and he veered off-course, noticing a door in the side of the building.

"Drop to the ground with your hands over your head!"

"Clear shot at the target, engaging!"

A barrage of gunfire. His shoulder was soaked with heat suddenly, his calf shredding itself so violently that he fell forward, screaming. The door was less than ten feet away – eight – and he surged forward desperately as another bullet tore through his

notrealnotrealnotrealnotrealnotreal

side.

"*I* am *fucking Brian Cooper!*" he yelled, and he was sure of it now. The door was close – he reached out to grab for the handle – another crack of thunder behind him, and the metal wall above exploded with a series of rapid-fire twangs. Louder than life. He fumbled with the handle, twisted it down, yanking the door back—

And as he did, he caught sight of his arm. The arm that had been shot off at the elbow, leaving him with a wet, bloody stump and a nub of bone.

For half a second he froze in the doorway, soldiers gaining on him from all sides, shoving their way through hordes of dreadful pale-skinned beasts, chaos exploding toward him from every direction.

The elbow had begun to lengthen, bone stretching and shearing through half-knitted clumps of pinkish, fleshy muscle. His forearm was a shrunken length of raw meat, the skin knotting into tight bundles and spreading. The cells had begun to work on forming fingers, and at the end of the weird stretched lump were five tiny nubs that wriggled as he stared blankly down at them.

"Oh my god," the clone whispered breathlessly, and then an explosion of gunfire rung in his ears and he panicked, bolting through the door and slamming it hard behind him.

PART IV

AN

OVERWHELMING

SURPLUS

OF

BRIANS

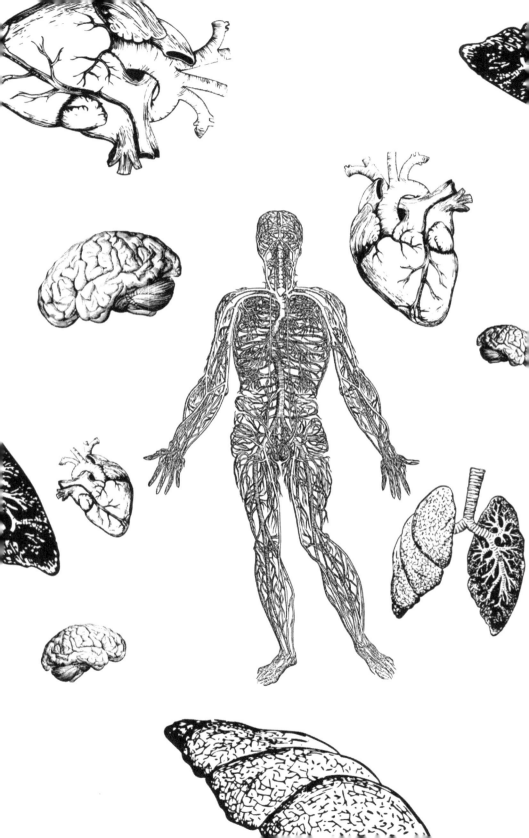

31

A single red light blinked slowly, the faint bloody spark of the bulb's worn-out filament a sizzling ember on the desktop that quickly burned out, only to reignite seconds later. It sat among a bank of similar bulbs, each one the size of a pinhead, thirty or so of them in total.

The only other light in the room came from a wall of monitor screens, hazy bands of black-and-white spooling across them and casting halos of grey on a far wall, upon which three wide corkboards had been decorated with maps and dull rusted pins.

After a few minutes the first blinking light was joined by another, this one right in the bottom corner of the panel. The two winked slightly off-time with each other, so that each dull ignition – always accompanied with a low, exhausted *bzzz* – was like a faint heartbeat. One, then the other half a second later, then darkness again.

Bzz-bzzz.

Bzz-bzzz.

Bzz-bzzz.

Something moved across the room, a lithe shape which had occupied a small pocket of shadow in the corner beside a pair of black filing cabinets. Each drawer was locked with a small electronic keypad; the tiny screen of each keypad flickered a dull red whenever those tiny lightbulbs reignited.

The shape bent over the desktop, glancing across the room toward the bank of monitors. Its face was sallow and old, its eyes nonetheless focused and clear. Thin stripes of shock-white lanced the dark hair at its temples.

The tall man watched the screens for a moment, then moved his hand toward the blinking red lights as if to smother them. His skin was weathered, the fingers long and bony.

Before he could turn out the lights, a third started to wink in unison:

Bzzzzz-bzz.

Bzzzzz-bzz.

"Well, what do you know?" the tall man said quietly to himself. Absent-mindedly he reached for a small switch on the side of the control panel and pressed it. All of the bulbs sizzled white-hot for a tiny portion of a second before dimming to orange and then dying completely. "Three of them in one night."

The hand moved to the tall figure's belt as he straightened up, his shadow looming over a dusty desktop that was otherwise scattered with blueprints and diagrams. A toppled cardboard Burger King cup had long since spilled its contents and the banana milkshake within had congealed into a thin drizzle of plasticky yellow that oozed off the edge of the table.

The tall man's finger hovered over a button on a bulky radio clipped to his waist. Just as he moved to jab the silicone button embedded in its casing, it crackled. A voice squawked at him:

"Sir, you may have seen. Incursion in the churchyard. Gunshots inside the church. Please advise."

The tall man's eyes moved to the screens across from him. Upon one of the monitors was a grainy image of the interior of the church: two figures lay limp on the floor, bloody lab coats strewn around them. The image might have been a still, at a glance, for the two women did not move. The things in the tanks behind them, however, squirmed excitedly.

"Sir? I've got a visual. One full-formed, headed for town."

Finally the tall man jabbed the button on his radio. He spoke softly,

150

his voice almost a whisper. "Turn him around," he said calmly. "Guide him to the Big Room."

"*But sir, we could—*"

"Yes," the tall man interrupted, "I'm quite certain you could. But I'd rather you do as you're told."

"*Yes, sir. What about the doors?*"

"I'll take care of the doors from here," the shape muttered. "Get your men into the churchyard. Rile up some of the half-forms, if you must. Get that incursion to the Big Room."

Before the soldier could reply, the tall man thumbed the button again.

"Oh, and don't try *too* hard to kill him, all right? Do what you must, but remember… remember, our boy likes to work for his food."

The tall man smiled, withdrawing into a narrow office chair and returning his attention to the monitors. Ignoring the response of the soldier on the other end of the two-way radio, he reached his long, slender fingers into the pocket of his coat and drew out a KitKat bar.

"Three in one night," he echoed, his eyes skitting from one screen to the next. Slowly he unravelled the chocolate bar and took a bite. "Unprecedented."

32

Thunder smashed into the great steel wall behind him, an unrelenting torrent of gunfire punching dents into the metal. Brian Cooper pressed his back to the door, sobbing uncontrollably as thick jets of pain seared his back, his side, his calf. His elbow twitched and buckled as the forearm he'd lost continued to slowly reform.

Voices behind the door. A female voice yelled: "*Hold your fire!*"

The thunderous reports of the semi-automatics slowed, finally pulling to a stop. The quiet that followed was worse. Outside the boy heard a scuffle, then the growl of one of the white-skinned half-creatures. Another brief burst of gunfire, then nothing.

More voices, close enough to the door that he could just about hear them, though it was evident they were trying to keep quiet.

"*—in there after him?*"

"*—no point... not coming out—*"

"*—if he tries to escape?—*"

—a bitter laugh—

"*—good luck to him...*"

The young man swallowed.

Taking a stumbling step forward, he looked about the room in which he'd found himself.

It was enormous.

The towering cylinder of steel behind the church was not, as he'd expected, another maze of corridors and locked rooms; instead it seemed to be the outer casing of one titanic silo. He stood at the edge of an arena the size of the coliseum, with walls taller than he could discern in the flickering half-light. There were three or four more doors around the extensive perimeter of the room, framed with plates of corrugated metal and thick concrete pillars. The floor was a great concrete circle hewn from the earth and scattered with a thick layer of dry white hay, as if some small collection of livestock had been stabled here. Gobs of manure littered the soft bedding, much of it dry and crumbling, some fresh and dark.

His eyes travelled up and he moved forward, gripping his softly-twitching forearm tightly. The bullet wounds in his side and leg seemed to have begun knitting together already, painfully forcing out the slugs; it was as though the realisation that his cells could heal like this had activated some urgency in their ability to do so. Or perhaps he had just stopped to breathe for long enough that he could finally feel something other than confusion and terror.

Above him, crooked wooden platforms poked out of the walls, supported by concrete struts. Lamps dangled from some, swinging softly and casting pale amber shadows onto curved banks of corrugated metal. He saw a door above one of the stands, and that the platform itself was bordered with tall iron railings, and decided it might have been some kind of observation platform. Thirty feet up, high enough to see the whole arena.

He limped forward.

A door squealed open suddenly, the other side of the arena, and something fell inside with a breathless, rasping urgency.

The boy's eyes dropped to the open door across the silo and he swallowed as it slammed shut behind the newcomer. His heart stopped in his chest as his eyes locked onto the thing that had hobbled in through the opening.

It looked back at him, its own eyes equally wide and horrified.

"Hello," the boy said hoarsely.

153

33

Cooper heard the thick, thundering report of semi-automatic rifle fire spraying the other side of the churchyard. Lurching out from his hiding place behind a leaning stone angel – her face broken so that all that remained was a lower jaw and a crumbling nose – he ran on aching legs into the shadow of the enormous silo around the back of the factory. The titanic building would provide the best shelter from whatever was shooting at him – or at something – he thought, dipping between gravestones as nausea broiled in his mouth.

He still had the ripe taste of soiled organic matter on his tongue and lining the back of his throat. He could feel a wriggling piece of Slackjaw's cartilage stuck between his teeth.

Somebody screamed, the other side of the silo. The thunder continued, smashing into the wall of the building and sending metallic booming ricochet twangs into the night. Cooper panicked, slamming his back against the wall and looking around.

Below him, he saw shapes rising from the fence around the churchyard, almost-human shapes with stubby limbs and smooth faces.

His eyes widened and he turned, looking for a door. He had to skirt around the building a little before he found one, sticking to the shadows, cringing as the awful things he'd eaten down in the sewer began to repeat in his stomach. Pealing with shame at his own savagery, he grabbed desperately for a rusted doorhandle and pulled.

The door was jammed. His heart leapt into his mouth as he wrenched it, struggling to heave open the door. Looking up, he saw a dim bar of red LEDs above the frame; he blinked, and when he looked again they were flickering yellow. After a moment they turned green, and he tried the handle again.

The door swung open and Cooper tumbled inside.

Apparently somebody was watching him.

Before he had time to process that information he was confronted with the smell of dry grass and manure and whirled around, his footstep echoing up the corrugated walls of the enormous room. The silo seemed to rattle as explosions smacked it from the outside.

He looked up and saw someone watching him from the other side of what appeared to be a massive, circular arena, dim bulbs swinging above him and illuminating wooden platforms jutting from the walls.

Cooper opened his mouth to say something, but his voice died in his throat. He squinted at the thing across the room, certain it couldn't be possible. He was imagining it. He was looking at…

Himself.

"Hello," said the other Brian, his own voice weak and timid but echoing loudly in the enormous silo. The gunfire outside had stopped, but Cooper noted that the mirror he was looking into reflected the wounds of somebody who hadn't quite managed to escape the bullets: the other him was ruined. Blood oozed in thick bands across his calf and ribboning tendrils that spread over his side and stomach. His hair was mussed and matted with blood, and his eyes burned with traumatised delirium. His right arm was a weird abomination of half-formed muscle and stubby fingers, slivers of bone showing between folds of pale skin that knitted together even as Cooper watched.

Brian Cooper – the savage who had waded through shit and blood, who had beaten attacking organs to pulp against the walls, who had eaten repugnant matter that was no doubt poisoning his insides even now – stared helplessly at the Brian Cooper in the other doorway.

The Brian Cooper who had found a stairwell underground, who had come out in the factory and found the truth – as terrible as it was – in the nave of a converted church, who had gripped tightly to hope right until this second and suddenly felt it dying and shrivelling into a ball in his stomach, stared right back.

"Hello," whispered Brian the Hungry.

"You look like shit," croaked Brian the Hopeful, noting the glossy wall of blood that coated the other Brian's chin and neck and spread half-congealed over his exposed chest. His legs and the entirety of his hospital gown were stained dark and covered with brown, tacky flecks, caked in muck and blood and exploded tissue.

"You don't look great," said the Hungry. "What the hell is this? What are you?"

"You haven't been to the church, I'm guessing."

"I came through the sewer. Found a ladder, came up above ground – somewhere in this creepy ghost town. There was gunfire… some mountainous cunt of a cowboy walking around, hunting something. Someone. I ran, ended up in the churchyard. Then… well, that's about it."

"Ghost town? What, the place at the bottom of the hill; you've been there?"

"Briefly."

There was a pause.

"So how are you… there?" the Hungry said, gesturing vaguely at the mirror image. Both of them had taken a couple steps into the arena, but neither were particularly eager to get much closer to their counterpart. "How are you me?"

"Cloning," the Hopeful said. He swallowed. "We're not real. We're clones."

"Clones. Right. And all the…"

"Organs?"

156

"Right," the Hungry nodded.

"Apparently cloning's difficult."

"Who knew?"

They laughed weakly, the sound odd and fragmented, two overlaid layers of near-identical ululation that echoed in the room and made both Brians feel a little queasy.

"So how do we—"

"—get out of here?"

Brian nodded. The other Brian shrugged.

"Speaking of *here*," Brian the Hopeful said, looking up and around, "what the hell is this?"

"Figured you'd know," Brian the Hungry said, following his doppelganger's gaze. "Being as you seem to have all the answers."

"I'll tell you all about it if we get out of here."

"Deal."

The Savage swallowed, grimacing at the taste of ruptured organ and shit as it repeated again in his throat. His eyes had locked on one of the wooden platforms above them, a curved plinth of rutting slats with thick supporting beams beneath and iron rods propping it up. A pair of lamps swung slowly above it, illuminating faint tufts of hay that drifted down, as if blown gently from a nest or a bed that something had made up there.

"What's that?" he whispered.

Before the other Brian could answer, the platform groaned with the great weight of something moving upon it. The Savage ducked back, suddenly somehow more afraid than he had been already.

The Hopeful sidled toward him, gulping hard.

"Whatever it is," he said, "it's waking up."

There was a dry *crunch* as a thick, twelve-fingered hand exploded forward and grabbed the edge of the platform, digging its chipped, bloody nails into the wood. The wrist was a mess of bony knobs and misplaced knuckles – a bracelet of them pushing up against thin, hairless skin – and the fingers were intertwined, enough for two-and-a-half hands bursting out of the palm of one.

Slowly the creature moved forward on the platform and looked down into the arena.

"Oh my god," said both Brians at once. "What the fuck is that?"

34

The entire silo seemed to groan as the creature slopped off its platform and onto the wall, moving like something gelatinous, something slug-like, despite all the limbs and bulging appendages thrusting out of its body.

The two Brians watched hopelessly as it revealed itself, a titanic mutant the size of an elephant – bigger, even – that seemed to be composed of a dozen or so bodies, each one spread into pieces and only vaguely human, fused together in one colossal mess of red and pink and dirty bone-white.

The thing looked at them hungrily with half of its faces, the others smeared against the wall. It half-crawled, half-dragged itself downward, leaving a thick trail of red with chunks and bits wriggling in it. The creature's bulk was a long misshapen cylinder of organic tissue, deflated lungs pinned to kidneys and livers and fused with long drooping trails of intestine that swung, twitching, like ropes off its gargantuan gut. Half-shattered, stubby ribcages were splayed open and pushed out of the membrane holding it all together, odd collections of yellowed bones forming haphazard spikes along what must have been the creature's back. It would have been impossible to count the amount of legs and arms that jutted from the creature's extremities and midsection – most of the legs, at least, seemed to be knitted to its undercarriage, while most of its arms flailed at the air and grabbed at the walls for anchorage. Here and there the odd one poked out in a nonsensical position – one leg, for example, thrust out through the open, silently-screaming mouth of one of the thing's many faces, and there were shallow red trenches in the flesh where the teeth had scraped it open. An arm was fused to another of the faces and the hand thrust back into the gobby red tissue behind its stumpy neck so that a right-angled elbow formed a huge, bony hindrance of an ear.

All the faces were Brian's. Presumably all of the organs and bones, too, though those were harder to identify. The grunting, gargling sounds that poured from half a dozen of its drooling mouths were odd corruptions of Brian's voice; the eyes that swung and rolled in their mutated, lumpen skulls were Brian's eyes.

The creature was a horrifying amalgamation of *him*.

It crashed to the floor, spraying tufts of hay into the air as it reared up like a sloppy, blood-and-mucus-coated centipede on its many legs. The arms jutting from its upper segments thrust out all at once, splaying into a halo of flexing, clawed fingers – some of those hands had only three or four, while some had up to twenty – and exposing the thing's belly. Groups of semi-fused organs pulsed and throbbed, bulging out of soft pink muscle striated with greasy yellow streaks. A bloated sac the size of a cow formed its belly, and inside – barely contained by the straining bloody membrane – was a network of body parts and pipes that didn't have any business connecting, and streams of blood and pus seemed to be squeezed from them every few seconds, spattering the inside of the sac.

"Fuck," Brian whispered.

"Fuck," Brian agreed.

The creature bellowed, half of its faces ripping open, mouths spreading wide as though the jaws were dislocated or broken. The sound was a ravenous echoing mess of gurgling, screaming voices, all of them coming from somewhere deep inside the creature's chest – or collection of chests, each one spread across its body.

Then it slumped forward, slamming dozens of hands into the ground and filling half the arena. Both Brians stumbled back; the Hungry grunted as his spine hit the wall and he glanced in the direction of the Hopeful, both of them sharing a terrified look.

One of the creature's faces licked its lips, eyes glinting greedily.

Suddenly there was a crackle high above them and Brian the Hopeful – becoming less so with every passing second – looked up, only noticing now a ring of speakers bracketed to the walls at the very top of the silo. A low, sardonic voice came through the speakers between bursts of static:

"—Good evening, boys. I must say, I've—*bzzzzt*—your little show, but—*bzzshk*—time for the main act."

"What the hell is this?" the Hungry yelled, looking desperately around for something to grab with which to arm himself.

"I never—*fshhkkkzz*—a son, you know. But I'd like—*sshkktt*—meet somebody who's become something—*bzzzzzztt*—family to me."

The creature swung its enormous globby shoulders from left to right and a few of its faces smiled proudly, their eyes blank and near-white.

"I call him *Carl*."

Brian the Hopeful gritted his teeth. "Oh, that's just sick."

The Hungry raised both hands. Speaking directly to the creature, he formed his words loudly and slowly: "You make me very uncomfortable!"

There came a high-pitched whine from the speakers and the creature baulked suddenly, rising up again onto its legs and spreading its arms wide – flaying them, the Hungry noted, like the hood of an agitated cobra. A face right in its centre seemed to grin gleefully, the eyes bright with recognition, the ears and hair fused into a bulging necklace of purplish organs. A ring of sharp bone-like protrusions surrounded the central head like a thorny white crown, many of them dripping with its own blood and translucent ropes of what looked like amniotic fluid.

Carl roared, all of its mouths opening at once and a thick, hungry explosion of sound punching outward into the silo. Then it bore forward hungrily, moving like water—

There was a dry, echoing report, the clap of a revolver, and the creature recoiled as a grisly red hole opened in its central face, the bones caving in with a series of wet cracks. It stumbled, its lumpen back slamming into the silo wall and shaking the whole building.

Both Brians looked back as a wisp of gunpowder smoke filtered into the arena.

A third Brian stood before them, gripping the blunt stock of a dusty Colt in both hands, eyes flitting from the Hungry to the Hopeful and then back to the creature.

Behind him, a door slammed shut. Above the frame a narrow bank of green LEDs went yellow, then red, as it locked.

"Hello," said Brian Cooper, lowering the revolver. "Either of you want to tell me what the hell's going on in here?"

35

Before Brian could explain where he'd gotten the gun, Carl had already begun to stir again.

"So there's three of us?" the Hungry yelled over the sloppy rumbling sound that echoed inside the silo.

"Maybe more," the Hopeful yelled.

Brian swallowed. He had woken up, not long ago, in that dreadful basement and quickly dressed himself in one of the gowns on the wall, stepping over and through mounds of wet and softly-squirming organs before heaving himself up the ladder and out into the square. He had glanced down as he climbed, and briefly wondered about the semi-human shape slouched against one wall and stirring; there had been something familiar about the shape but as it started forward he had panicked and let the lid close, stumbling back.

If only he'd seen its face...

Haunted by the ghostly white shapes in the ghost town beneath the churchyard, he had carried the Colt through the dark tunnels of the factory until he came to a door marked in slick, red paint. It had unlocked at his touch, and now he was here. Three of him were here.

"Three of us," Brian the Haunted agreed. "One of... that."

The Hopeful turned back toward the monster, shaking his head as it writhed and convulsed onto its feet. Great ropes of blood swung from

Carl's shattered skull, the others screaming and twisting, straining the bunched lashings of muscle and intestine that anchored them in place. "We need to get out," he said.

"Soldiers outside," said Hungry Brian. "Underground?"

"If we can find a way," said Hopeful Brian.

"Back through the factory, maybe," Haunted Brian offered.

There was no time to argue; before any of them could make another suggestion, the abomination had hauled its tacky, pulsing belly off the floor and it was swinging at them, dozens of arms swiping through the air as it bellowed hungrily.

36

The creature yelled, its entire body rippling upward as it reared over the three Brians. There was a moment where the absolute terror of all three pulsed so violently into the room that it seemed to become some invisible, pregnant sac in the air, throbbing around the many-headed upper half of the abomination.

Then it surged forward, ripping through the thin membrane of that sac and spilling all that awe and dread into the Big Room like waves of warm, wet blood.

Brian saw the creature crashing toward him and yelped, raising his mutilated arm to cover his face. A split-second later, remembering that the still-forming nub of lumpen muscle wouldn't do him much good, he raised his good arm and formed a sort of cross in front of his eyes; in the next moment the creature was upon him and he felt three dozen mismatched fingers rake the flesh of both arms, drawing deep bloody gouges through his flesh. There was another bellowing roar and he felt hot, ripe breath wash over his face; unable to stop himself from cringing, he turned his head to see that the other him – the one with the gun – had been punched right into the wall by the impact of a slopping sac of ropey organs at the creature's waist. The rubbery, wet sac quivered, dripping and indented where it had smashed into the boy's face.

The third Brian – the one who'd only recently escaped the sewers, where the only other signs of life had been undead organs and one bony, rasping hunk of skull and spine – ducked beneath a swinging pair of arms, fused at the elbow, and wheeled around the creature's side. He gazed up at the mountain of Carl's back and swallowed. The red-and-pink-streaked slope of torn muscle and bulbous, throbbing pieces of flayed organ lurched away from him in a swaying, segmented nightmare of wet flesh. He grimaced and leaped forward.

The other side of the creature, Brian staggered away from the wall and raised his revolver, briefly eyeing the chamber to see how many rounds were still locked inside. His vision was swimming but he knew that the gunslinger had given it to him fully-loaded and that he had fired one shot into one of the creature's heads… did that leave him with five? Had he forgotten something?

Swallowing, he lifted his arm and fired again.

The blast of the gun sent a small shockwave into his wrist and the sound echoed in his ears long after the bullet had smacked the creature somewhere in the top right – he couldn't call it a shoulder, or a part of the thing's chest, because Carl was so shapeless and fluid that it was just… an unknowable part of it – and sunk into the soft folds of a pair of kidneys fused to each other, and to a wider blob of yellow intestine flattened around them. Moments later the sunken kidneys blossomed again like the leaves of a flower in heat, spitting out the mangled bullet. He fired a second time and the next round punched into one of the creature's legs, the sharp report of the Colt accompanied by a shrill, whistling scream.

The Brian with the mutilated forearm finally wrangled it free of Carl's grip and, before the creature could whip its arms back to strike again, he pounced forward and grabbed the nearest one with both hands – one stubby and largely useless, the other drenched with a glossy coat of blood – and yanked the arm at the elbow. There was a dry *snap* as the arm splintered, a spike of bone shearing through flesh and winging blood. The abomination yowled, smacking another of its hands into Brian's neck and grabbing both the boy's arms with three of its own.

Behind the creature the third Brian slammed his foot into the creature's abdomen – or, at least, the squishy mass of pulsing organs that made up for a section of its abdomen – and launched himself upward. The creature's back was slippery but he managed to knot his fingers around a titanic disc of spinal column that poked itself out of the fleshy tissue. The bone was slippery with scraps of cartilage but he gripped hard, using the crude handhold to heave himself upward. Grabbing another disc of vertebrae he roared with agony as the creature shuddered beneath him. Legs and body caked with sewage, he began to climb.

Another report of the Colt and the creature buckled forward. Taking advantage of the sudden swell of gravity, the climbing boy scrambled upward, heading for the mess of bony spines that thrust out of the thing's upper back.

"What are you doing?" yelled another of the Brians, wrangling his body free of the creature's grip and plunging his stubby mutilated arm into the sac of mucus and organs swinging at its waist. Finding something wet and round he clenched his fist and wrenched it out, a spray of pink fluid covering his face. "You'll fall!"

A lashing tentacle of intestine exploded from the abomination's midsection and thrashed in the other Brian's direction, punching the revolver out of his hand. It skittered across the floor and the boy lunged for it, yelling in dismay. Another ribbon of coiled tissue smashed the side of his face and he staggered, swiping at empty air.

Sewage dripped from Brian's gown as he leapt upward, wrapping both of his arms around a thick, knotted spike of bone swinging out of Carl's back. Here there was a thicket of them, a rippling mass of spines punching out of the matter between the creature's shoulders; he gripped it tight and grunted as the creature swung its body again, his legs slipping and dangling free. A wall of vertigo flattened him against the bloody ruin of the abomination's spine. "Fuck!"

The boy with the messed-up arm looked up, the wriggling stump of his nearly-whole hand coated in amniotic fluid. For a frantic half-second he wondered if he should let Carl toss the dangling Brian to his death – after all, what the hell were they going to do after this?

There was only one Mrs Cooper. Only one Josh.

The three of them couldn't *all* make it out of here.

"No," he muttered to himself, shaking off the thought immediately after it had entered his brain. They were all in this together. They *had* to make it out.

Especially if none of them were the real thing.

Across the arena, Brian fumbled with the gun and swiped it into his palm, slamming down the hammer. Two shots left. He swung his arm around and aimed, holding his breath; three of the creature's faces turned to glare at him and he squeezed his eyes shut, pressuring the trigger blindly.

There was a *crack* and a wheeze and when he opened his eyes again one of those faces was gone, a massive hole in its centre. Where the ragged black hole should have been filled with chunks of brain matter, thick tendons whipped about, like the head's brains had been replaced by wiry snakes.

A thick wet weight crashed into his back as the creature lashed out with a malleable section of its body. Brian tumbled to his knees, dropping the gun again. Carl growled loudly above him and he looked up, his eyes flitting from the Brian with the messed-up arm to the one desperately clinging to one of the bony protrusions shivering out of the abomination's back.

Leave them, whispered a voice in his head. *Get out of here.*

"No," he groaned, climbing to his feet. Immediately another twisted knot of intestine-tentacles whipped outward and swung hard into his side, smashing him into the wall. Black clouds clotted his vision as agony rippled up his side.

High above, Brian locked his ankle around another of the creature's bony spines and screamed as knobs of muscle elongated and punched him in the gut, wetly smacking his arms, trying to bat him away. A face close to him hissed loudly and a too-long tongue lolled out from between blue lips, twisting and writhing. The eyes rolled up.

He looked down. One of his clones (*Brian's* clones, he remembered

168

bitterly – *just like you*) was on the floor and clutching desperately at his gut, the gun a few feet out of his reach. The other was screaming as the creature clamped the teeth of one of its many heads over his good wrist.

He could climb his way out of here, he thought as the creature swung its body and he flew briefly through the air. Grabbing another spike, he wrestled his way up onto Carl's meaty wet shoulder and stumbled dizzily, his foot sinking into a pit of soft, discoloured bladder. The others would be fine. And if not… well, he might not have any more right to Brian Cooper's life than either of them, but he still *had* a right to it.

Why not him? After all, the three of them couldn't share a life.

"No!" he roared, wrestling his way to the creature's neck and plunging both hands inside. He grabbed for a lump of bone, something solid, anything he could wrench out and swing into the nearest of the abomination's faces; nothing. There was a network of interconnected, mutated spines somewhere in there, but…

The creature staggered backward suddenly and he grabbed at a nest of tendril-like tendons in its neck, clinging on for dear life. Was it injured, or shocked? No, this was deliberate, he realised as the creature slammed its back into the wall; it was trying to shake him off—

He yelled as a tendon snapped hard in his hand and he fell, knocking his skull on a bone-spike on the way down to the floor. Vertigo rushed him again as the air tipped upward and he smashed into a cloud of hay with a bolt of pain.

Meanwhile the Brian with the broken arm yanked it out of the monster's vice-like jaws and looked around. Both the others had been floored, one of them winded and grabbing at his chest, the other badly bruised and rolling onto his stomach.

"Shit," Brian said, looking up into the yawing expanse of the creature's red, raw horror.

It lunged for him and he screamed as he lunged right back, the arena exploding with a bloom of hay and blood as he launched himself, alone, at the abomination's gut.

37

The tall man sat comfortably in his narrow office chair, his face bathed in the flickering glow of the monitors on the wall across from him. Lights blinked on a small panel somewhere behind his head.

Crunching up the KitKat wrapper, he tossed it absent-mindedly into a waste bin across the room. "Come to watch the show?" he called.

The shadow in the doorway seemed to melt out of the wall and it stepped forward, a mountain of patchwork darkness. "You enjoy this too much," it said.

The tall man smiled thinly, withdrawing another chocolate bar from his coat and offering it to the intruder. "Twix?"

"I thought I killed you a long time ago," the gunslinger growled, stepping into the faint, flickering light of the screens. The wide brim of his hat obscured his eyes, but his gritted teeth flashed in the dark. His leather coat stunk of blood and grit.

"You might have killed one of me," the tall man smiled slyly.

"You're a smug prick, ain't you?" the cowboy snarled, glancing sidelong at the man in the chair. "How many of the people working for you know you're still alive?"

"Those that need to."

The gunslinger straightened up, towering over the man in the chair. Where the latter was slender and bony, the gunslinger was a beast of thick muscle and thicker leather. "I've had enough of this," he said quietly. He gestured to the monitors. Upon one of the screens, three vague shapes ducked and swelled as a larger, formidable blot of pixels swiped hungrily at them. "We all have."

The tall man smiled. Standing from the chair, he moved to the nearby desk, appearing to scour some of the scattered documents briefly. Sniffling, he tucked the Twix back in his coat and turned to grin back at the gunslinger. "It's not up to you to decide when this is done," he said flatly. His hand moved subtly to the panel behind him and he gently pressed a small grey switch. Pressed it twice, for good measure.

Signal sent, he returned to the chair.

"Good boy," the gunslinger said, producing a long-barrelled revolver from his coat. Softly he thumbed the hammer. The *click* echoed throughout the half-lit room.

"Thought you gave that to the boy?" the tall man said quietly.

The cowboy grimaced. "You're not the only one who likes to keep a spare."

Without waiting for the tall man to reply, the gunslinger raised his arm and squeezed the trigger. The bullet smacked the tall man right between the eyes with a dull *clap*, punching a deep black hole in his cranium and smashing out through the back of the office chair. The chair rocked with the impact; already blood was oozing slowly from the wound. Thin ribbons of brain matter dribbled down the chair and onto his back as he limply flopped forward, eyes rolling up in his head.

The cowboy turned to the monitors. His eyes moved to a screen in the top left and he watched the gritty silhouetted figurines of a dozen soldiers running across the churchyard, turning away from the titanic metal silo and barrelling downhill, torchlights swinging on the ends of thick, bulky rifles.

Coming toward him.

His eyes shifted to the control panel on the desk, where a white light blinked slowly.

"Shit," he said.

38

Brian grabbed a clump of curved ribcage and heaved himself one-handedly up the beast's abdomen, slamming his knee into a rippling tumour of fused spleen and kidney. It popped wetly in his face and he howled, yanking down on the ribs like a knotted lever and wrenching them out of the thing's body. It wailed and swiped at him; ducking his head, Brian slammed his stump-hand into the creature's stomach – one of them, at least, semi-visible beneath a thin membrane of raw skin – and squeezed.

Across the Big Room, Brian's eyes snapped open. The silo swum around him as he wheeled onto his feet, grabbing at the wall for support with one sewage-covered hand. Nausea surged up his body, threatening to bring up chunks of Slackjaw and the other awful things he'd eaten down in the tunnels. His gaze locked onto the body across the room: another Brian lay on the floor, his eyes rolled up in his head, his body twitching with agony.

As the boy lurched in the other Brian's direction he realised something: he had seen them both before. When he'd woken up in the basement... Christ. He'd heard the manhole cover shutting above him, known that *something* had gone up that ladder. He'd missed this Brian by seconds. And the other one... the monstrous, bent figure he'd glimpsed by the staircase. Had he climbed right up into the factory?

If they'd all just waited, could they have fought their way through this together? Could they be out of here by now?

He crumpled, crouching by the other Brian's side and shaking him anxiously. "Come on…"

Above them, the third Brian had locked his arms around one of Carl's growling heads and was wrenching at its neck, trying desperately to pull it off. Wet flecks of meat sprayed the floor as flesh began to strain and tear.

Brian opened his eyes and looked up at the Brian crouching over him. "You thought about leaving us here," he whispered. "Thought you could be"—a pained grunt, and he rolled onto his back—"the only one."

Brian shook his head. "How did you—"

Brian grinned. "So did I."

Brian looked up. "D'you think he—"

"Probably," Brian said.

"But we wouldn't," Brian said firmly. "We're all getting out of here."

"Same conclusion I came to," Brian grunted.

"Funny, that."

They laughed weakly. Behind them a great weight shuddered into the wall of the silo, the whole cylindrical tower shaking violently.

"Wait here," the sewage-covered Brian said, helping the other to his knees before lurching away. He limped awkwardly to the wall, slamming his body into the door. He grabbed for the handle and pulled it frantically, wrestling with it in the rusted mechanism. "It's locked!" he called back.

"Thought it might be," the other Brian grunted, rolling forward and swiping at his gun. He grabbed it and pointed, eyes moving to the chamber. One shot left.

Far above them the Brian with the ruined arm screamed, finally ripping Carl's head off and letting it drop to the floor. A jet of blood shot out of the hole, followed by a wriggling mass of tendon-tendrils that grabbed at the edges of the wound and tried to pull it in. Brian

174

slipped, grabbing a jutting chunk of bone and slamming both his feet into another of the big beast's faces.

"This one too!" came a yell from beneath him. He glanced down and saw his doppelganger wrestling with a door across the room, then running to another. "Fuck, they're all locked!"

On the ground, Brian nodded grimly. "Yeah," he said, flexing his knuckles around the stock of the Colt. "There's only one way out of here."

He raised the gun high and fire off a round with an almighty *smack*.

The bullet punched into a wooden support beam above the creature's head. Rotting wood exploded and the platform that had been propped up on the beam fell, swinging downward. It smashed into the creature's upper body, slamming two of its heads and punching a lump of bone deep into the neck-like collection of parts that the third Brian was clinging to.

The creature stumbled back, clearly overwhelmed by pain. As its back smashed into the wall Brian fell, losing his one-handed grip and tumbling to the floor.

"Fuck you!" the Brian who'd spent his time in the tunnels yelled, turning away from the locked door and launching himself at one of the creature's legs. He clamped his teeth into flesh and ripped, tearing away a great hunk. The beast seemed to have recovered from the impact of the collapsing platform and he kicked out, lashing at the attacking savage beneath him.

The other Brians shared a defeated look. The doors were locked. The bullets were gone. The creature was unkillable.

This was it.

Across the arena, Carl slammed a bony knee into Brian's stomach and knocked him back into the wall. Winded, the boy wheezed and a thick gob of blood drooled out of his mouth.

The creature turned toward the others, grinning with two of its remaining heads while the others healed themselves, skin fusing back together, new chunks of muscly armour already forming over holes in its body.

Brian looked up at the speakers far above them and screamed, "*Open these fucking doors!*" but nobody was listening, not anymore.

There was no way out.

39

The cowboy watched the carnage on three of the two-dozen monitors before him, his eyes flitting from one to the other beneath the shadowy brim of his hat. Behind him in the office chair, a thin line of blood oozed out of the tall man's mouth.

The gunslinger's thumb hovered open a small grey switch. Just beneath it on the desk, a sticker had been adhered that read *Silo Doors 1-3 lock/unlock*.

He hesitated.

There was a sudden burst of movement on one of the screens to the top right of the bank and his gaze shifted upward. He watched as twenty-or-so soldiers stormed across a band of shifting static grains. He could hear them outside now, thumping footsteps booming through the walls of the darkened room.

"Shit-fucker," he growled, withdrawing his thumb from the button. Sparing the monitors one last glance, he tipped his hat semi-ceremonially and turned to leave.

40

"Wait!" Brian yelled, stumbling onto his feet. Across the arena, the others looked blankly at him. He ignored them, staggering toward the creature. "Wait! Listen to me!"

"What are you doing?" Brian hissed.

Gritting his teeth, Brian took another step and looked up into the abomination's closest face. A twisted distortion of his own face gazed sleepily down at him, one of its eyes pulsing; beside the socket, a lumpen mass of gall bladder had been fused to its skull. This shrivelled and inflated in rhythm, shrivelled and inflated again, as it listened.

"Why are we fighting?" Brian yelled. "We're all the same!"

"Oh, this is dumb," whispered the other two Brians.

"You can hear me, right?" he called up. Carl shivered, its whole body trembling wetly. "You can understand me? I know you... you don't want to be trapped here like this, right? You're me! You're *us*!"

"That's true," Brian murmured. Beside him, Brian nodded. One of them called up: "He's right! We could get out of here together!"

The first Brian nodded. "You help us get out of here, and we'll find you somewhere better! We could find you a home! You don't have to live in this... this fucking oversized tin can any more!"

He glanced at the other Brians. Something passed unspoken between them, something silent.

They agreed.

"We just need to get out of this door," the last Brian yelled, pointing, "and then we can take you away! That's all, all right? Just... help us with the door!"

"Just the door," another Brian whispered.

"Come on..."

Carl seemed, impossibly, to be considering it for a moment. Then the creature surged forward, slamming its upper body wormlike into the ground and rearing its heads up, splaying its arms again in a violent display of size. It loomed over the Brian who had spoken first, the Brian who had staggered through a mess of gore in the tunnels and come up above ground to find *this* waiting for him. He squeezed his eyes shut and backed up against the wall, heart thudding in his chest, entire body shaking. This was it. It was going to fucking chew him up and spit him out.

He wondered how many times that would happen to him before the scientists finally decided to incinerate his remains.

"Help you," three of the thing's heads croaked as one, "help me."

Brian's eyes snapped open. He shivered. He had heard those words before. And he had eaten the thing that had spoken them.

"Help me, help you," he whispered, his eyes flitting to the nearby Brians then back to Carl. Swallowing, he nodded toward the nearest door and said, "Get us out of here."

41

The churchyard was quiet, a broiling slope of grieving shadows in which only slow shapes crawled. Many of the half-forms had returned to the abandoned town below, and most of the guards had gone to deal with the incursion in Arnett's old office.

Only a few of them were permitted to know who worked there now – who ran this whole complex – but they all knew that he was just as integral to it as Arnett had been. And if one of the clones had gotten in there...

"You two doing anything after this?" one of the remaining guards said quietly, looking lazily about the cemetery. The crashing and booming inside the silo had stopped, but he hoped to give it a few more minutes before they went in to recover the scraps the creature had left. None of them liked to enter the Big Room while he was still hungry.

Across from him, a woman shrugged, her semi-automatic jerking in her arms. Casually she batted a white-skinned stalker off her arm and shook her head. "Not much. Back to work tomorrow night, think I'll just take a long nap."

"You, Robbie?" said the first guard.

The third grinned, his eyes hidden beneath the black curve of his visor. His teeth flashed in the dark. "You know that new *Legend of Zelda* that came out the other week? Finally convinced the missus to let me grab a Switch so I can play that bad boy."

"Oh, yeah?"

"Shit, yeah. I love all that."

The woman beside him grunted. "Nerd."

"Yeah, well, I didn't get to do that shit when I was a kid, you know?"

"That's fair. I always preferred—"

The doorway nearest to them exploded and the entire silo wall buckled outward, mangled belts and wreaths of metal rupturing in a great ragged eruption of sound. The closest guard turned his head and the man with the bright white teeth staggered back, the woman swinging her rifle around immediately. Her eyes widened as the abomination barrelled out of the Big Room, roaring out of multiple mouths as it pounded legs and arms into the ground, lurching toward them in a bloody streak of red.

42

"Down!" Brian yelled, grabbing the others and yanking them back by their gowns.

A clacking report of semi-automatic rifle fire exploded into the night, ripping apart the creature in seconds. Bullets flew through quivering organs and tore great strips and ribbons of flesh from the bulk of its body, spraying it in bright red chunks against the silo wall.

The abomination roared, its whole body splaying upward and out as it reared up, its movements interrupted by the thunderstorm of metal flaying it open. The gunfire seemed to slow as it rocked in the air, then – after a terrible, eternities-long second – fell forward and crumpled into the earth.

The cemetery shuddered as Carl fell passed-out and convulsing to the ground.

He wouldn't be down for long.

Sheltering from the gunfire behind the enormous creature's body, the first Brian looked up. His eyes locked onto the second as he swayed, clutching his neck.

"No…"

The second Brian looked at him, smiling weakly. Thin dribbles of red oozed between his fingers, then as his hand began to shake and the pressure on his neck grew softer, it pumped out in thick ropes of red and he fell. A stray bullet had clipped him right in the carotid artery; his blood splashed the grass as he swayed onto his belly, eyes rolling up in his head.

"No!" the first Brian yelled, crawling over frantically. He hooked one hand under the second Brian's neck and clamped the other over the wound, blood covering him immediately. Only now that the wet heat of the fluid splashed him did he realise his skin was stiff and covered with goosebumps; he wondered ridiculously just how cold it was out here. He briefly registered that his own stomach had been shot, and thought he could feel at least three holes spewing hot pain across his side.

The third Brian lurched to one side as one of the three soldiers saw him and launched another burst of gunfire. He ploughed forward and slammed his body into the guard's midsection, knocking him down and wrestling for the rifle. Locking his fingers around the soldier's arm he slammed an elbow into the man's chin and pointed the gun across Carl's twitching, titanic body.

A spray of bullets hit the female guard in the mouth and her face exploded, teeth punched back into her helmet. The rifle slammed Brian's elbow and he yelled as he continued to compress the trigger, tilting the barrel in the third guard's direction before he could raise his own weapon. The soldier's chest turned to ribbons and mist.

Still yelling, he yanked the rifle out of the soldier's arms and turned his body around, swinging the thing in a vicious arc across the man's midsection. The guard squeaked as his stomach was ripped to shreds and he was blown back into the nearest headstone.

The abomination moved suddenly, one powerful convulsion sending it rolling onto one side and swinging with all its arms at once. A couple caught the first Brian in the face and he yowled as his right eyeball turned to pain, hot jelly splashing his cheek. He tumbled back into the silo wall.

"No," the third Brian whispered, turning the rifle on Carl and preparing to fire.

But the abomination was still, that last convulsion just a gargantuan death throe. It was over now.

He looked toward his brothers and cringed. One lay on the floor, his neck a mess of raw red meat, his chest heaving as he drew in gargling breaths. The other's face had a great red trench raked out of it, one eye missing, and his stomach was pumped with gory red holes. Both of them looked pathetic and broken; he didn't imagine he looked much better.

The churchyard was quiet. The creature was down – for now – and the guards had all miraculously disappeared, off on some other violent errand. They could escape. They could make it out of here.

They were free.

They were done. But…

But it wasn't right.

What's the fucking point?

He felt dreadful. His body was broken, his mind swimming in a soup of confusion and horror. The others were in a similar state, both of them slowly dying on the floor. He fancied once the adrenaline had worn off he might just fall down dead himself.

And what was there to go home for? If the scientists had been telling the truth…

"Fuck," he whispered.

Slowly, he looked down at the rifle. He had no idea how much was left in it, but he had to hope there was something.

He glanced across toward the other Brians. The one with the ruined neck had gone still; the other was watching him.

"We're all thinking it, right?" the two of them said weakly.

Around them the churchyard shuddered gently, the cool night air dreadful and calm.

Grimacing, Brian nodded. "We'd heal, you know," he whispered. "Given enough time. We could all three of us get out of here."

The Brian with the messed-up stomach smiled sadly. "What's the point?" he said.

"Don't say that."

"But what is there for us? There might be enough out there for one

184

of us to scrape together some kind of life… not three of us."

"Come on," Brian said, looking down at the rifle in his hands. "Don't make me do this."

"It's okay," the other Brian croaked, blood pumping out of his belly at an alarming rate. "Just… do… it…"

He went still.

"No…"

Brian half-heartedly raised the rifle. He had meant to make their suffering shorter. Meant to end it, right here and now.

Instead he had wasted the last few minutes of his own life.

He closed his eyes and turned the rifle upward, gripping it hard with both hands and slamming the barrel into his chin. The metal was hot. Burning.

Sobbing, he rested two fingers on the trigger and prepared to send a rocket of gunfire into his skull.

The shadows swelled around him. *Three. Two. One…*

"Fuck," he said, dropping the rifle.

Then he screamed, one long primal bellow coming from deep within his stomach. Staggering back, he crashed into a tilted gravestone and wheeled around, roaring at the churchyard around him before tumbling downhill into the dark.

43

It wasn't long before he stopped, heaving, at the bottom of the hill, his aching body drenched in the shadow of a tall skeletal watchtower. He sobbed uncontrollably into the grass, splaying his fingers in the earth and howling in agony between choked breaths. Eventually, he stopped. It was impossible to tell how much time had passed, but it might only have been minutes.

It felt like it could have been the majority of the remainder of his life.

Another shadow fell across him and he looked up, eyes filled with blood. Swaying in the grass, he moaned, "What have I done? I just left them there... I was going to – oh, god, we were so *close...*"

The gunslinger stood silently for a moment, his enormous body a silhouette in the moonlight. Somewhere behind him, a thick band of blood-red was seeping slowly across the horizon: the first traces of sunlight. A brand new day.

After a minute the cowboy crouched, still looming over the boy, the folds of his leather coat pooling around him in the grass. "Got your answers then, huh?" he said quietly.

Brian nodded, tears streaming into all the blood on his face and down into the ground at his knees. "I have to... I've got to go and find my mum. Find... Josh."

The gunslinger's head bowed forward and Brian noted that the big man was rocking on his heels, not enjoying this any more than he was. This seemed almost painful for him. "I did that," the man whispered. "Nearly thirty years ago, I did that."

"You—"

"They've moved on, Brian. Things ain't the same out there as they was, you know. For us, or anyone else."

Brian swallowed. He'd known, but he hadn't thought about it. Hadn't had time. It was the shape of the man's face, the way his voice – aged and depressed – still carried the same speech patterns.

"You want to get out of here?" the cowboy said.

Brian shook his head. "What's the point?"

"I don't know, kid."

"I don't deserve... I'm not even real. I'm not even *human*, am I?"

"You're real, kid, but you're not him. You're gonna have to make yourself a new life out there."

"I can't..."

"Then here's your choice," the gunslinger said, and suddenly there was a Colt in his hand, identical to the one he had given Brian. Gently, he thumbed the hammer.

Brian's breath hitched in his throat.

"You tell me what's kinder," the gunslinger said softly, thumbing the hammer, "and I'll do it."

A silence fell between them, heavy as the grave. Eventually Brian said, "Was she okay? Did she... did she ever get away from him?"

"She didn't," the gunslinger said flatly. Then he gestured vaguely with the revolver. "But I took care of him."

"I reckon that's what I'd do," Brian said. He laughed humourlessly. Then the laughter turned to more tears and he broke down, clamping both hands over his head and pulling himself down into the dirt.

"Tell me what you want," the gunslinger whispered. "Tell me what'd be kinder, and I'll do it for you. The choice is yours."

Brian looked up, looked right down the barrel. "You're me," he said. "You're the only me that was ever real. You... *you* know what'd be kinder."

"Yeah," the gunslinger said sadly. "I was afraid you were going to say that."

Behind them, rain began to filter into the ruptured silo and a small crowd of black-clad soldiers tramped their way up through the churchyard, swinging torch beams around and illuminating the headstones.

Somewhere below ground, a gritty pair of eyes snapped open and something gasped in a breath of stale, stinking air.

Also available
from the author:

Day of the Mummy
Night of the Bunny
Dark Nights
Dead Engines
Moondisc
Empire of Cold
Drop Bear
Parliament of Witches
Burrow

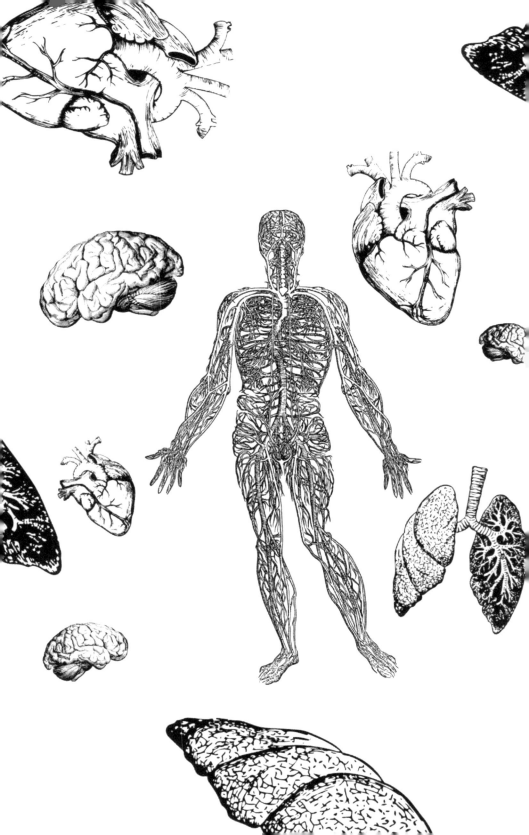

9 781915 272904